AUTUMN

AUTUMN

A. G. Mojtabai

1982
Houghton Mifflin Company   Boston

Library of Congress Cataloging in Publication Data

Mojtabai, A. G., date
  Autumn.

  I. Title.
PS3563.O374A97   813'.54   81-23523
ISBN 0-395-32051-8   AACR2

Printed in the United States of America

S   10 9 8 7 6 5 4 3 2 1

The author gratefully acknowledges permission to quote the poem
"Winter Is Another Country" from *New and Collected Poems
1917–1976* by Archibald MacLeish. Copyright © 1976 by Archibald
MacLeish. Reprinted by permission of Houghton Mifflin Company.

For Jack

If the autumn would
End! If the sweet season,
The late light in the tall trees would
End! If the fragrance, the odor of
Fallen apples, dust on the road,
Water somewhere near, the scent of
Water touching me; if this would end
I could endure the absence in the night,
The hands beyond the reach of hands, the name
Called out and never answered with my name:
The image seen but never seen with sight.
I could endure this all
If autumn ended and the cold light came.
—ARCHIBALD MacLEISH
"Winter Is Another Country"

The author wishes to express gratitude to the staff of the library at Southwest Harbor, Maine, for their great courtesy and helpfulness.

Contents

I

Rounds

THEY ARE pulling the pleasure boats up out of the water. Back to the long shed for winter. You are five months gone. You'd hardly know the summer's over. It's wild and blowy out, but kind of quiet, there's a smell of mown grass, a ripe green smell still, the heat, pressed down all summer long, now beating upwards from the earth, something golden in the air. All pointless without you.

I never stayed on past Labor Day before. Always thought how fine it would be to be able to. It's not the way I pictured it, though; not like this. I never planned on staying on alone.

That must have been the last of the tourists I saw yesterday, that old couple, the old man with the Polaroid camera. He was taking a picture of his Missus eating a lobster on the pier, as if she'd done something to be proud of. The people from the summer cottages have all gone by, leaving a lot of space. Heaps of quiet. On Harbor Street, the beads and basket places are open, but idling; everything's discount now. There's a sign on the door of Samantha's Sandals and Leatherworks:

TIRED
Closed today
Open Saturday

That quiet, now, it's so thick you can taste it, I swear.
But rounding the corner near Pleasant Street, I pick up
my ears. Something going on . . . Pass the Baptist church and
stop a minute: it's coming from somewhere else. Pass Mount
Heartworn Methodist — it isn't here. It's still coming, this
heavy *tock, tock* —

And then I see. On the porch of Dew Drop Inn, two
rocking chairs are going at it, teetering up and down, chatting and nodding in the breeze. It gives me a real eerie feeling: not a soul in them. The Vacancy sign is out and that's
creaking, too. It's warm in the sun, gold and warm.

Step into Mullins' store and aren't things humming
there! The place is full of the old folks loitering about,
fumbling the bread, poking the tomatoes, reading the cans.
FRIENDLIEST STORE IN TOWN. I pick up the paper that
tells me what's on sale. Tuna fish is reduced today. Aisle 3.
Sixty-nine cents. FABULOUS BUY. Franco-American spaghetti is on sale. Kraft instant macaroni. SUBSTANTIAL
SAVINGS. Aisle 5. I am in aisle 7 and 8. Is it 7? Or 8? I,
too, am much reduced. I am not such a fabulous buy. I
amuse myself, but not really, only for half a minute at most.
Catch myself chatting all the time, it's in my mind, sometimes joking, but mostly bellyaching — don't know who to.
To Helen, of course, that's habit — but who besides? It's
the damndest thing, because I've never been a talker, not
a bit sociable. It always was a problem for me.

Mullins is stacking up the mustard and pickles as I go by
and his radio's going strong. It's a song — I can only make
out the words here and there. The background is brassy,
loud. "Nice out," I say. "Come again?" says Mullins.
"Pretty day," I raise my voice a little. He agrees it's pretty
fair.

I come in every morning just about now and it's always
just like this. Except for Saturdays, I never do shopping for

more than a day at a stretch. I like to come in here, it gives me something to do. Same with the others. Somebody asks: "How are you, Tom?" "Better than nothing," Tom says. "Didn't I see you here yesterday?" And the other: "Got to eat every day, don't I?" It's the same.

Ketchup, can of tuna — two, while I'm at it, they're such a good buy. Can of Franco-American spaghetti. Can of baked beans. It's hard finding the right size; most everything's packed for two. Ever try buying one cupcake? It can't be done.

I go round the breads. The place is buzzing, like I say. On top of this, Mullins' radio is going a mile a minute. I can make out about half the words now. Not that it matters. It's one of those hit-parade songs and they're all about love — finding it, losing it, finding it for real, for ever and ever. If I've heard one, I've heard them all:

> My tears are falling cause . . .
> (*Can't hear it, can't hear it*)
> Take good care of my baby
> Now don't you ever make her cry . . .
> (*Some something, do something* —)

Maybe? Baby? Can't hear it.

Can't make it out. I buy a pack of chocolate cupcakes (a pair, that's the smallest), can of beer, can of chicken soup, milk, sugar. Eggs? I open up a half-carton and check that none are cracked, then remember I don't need any. One tomato. Lettuce a little limp today — I'll wait.

That should do it for now. Ah, slow here. Here's the checkout. The woman in front of me holds a fistful of coupons. She's humming to the music, I can make out a little. "Now don't you ever . . . ." Then I lose it. This should take some time. Fine by me. I stare at the cashier.

The girl looks up, seems to smile at me. Or maybe she's

just clamping down on her chewing gum a second, I'm not sure. She chews so hard. Her eyes turn on me, of that I'm sure; I feel them move: a very white light.

Looks away, the light is gone.

She's different from the others. Slower, sulkier, superior; the job (she feels it) drags at her more. She's not from here — one day I heard her say. Her name's Sue. It's on her smock, that's how I know. I always try and choose her lane, so I suppose she recognizes me by now. Or does she? No way of telling, really, I don't know beans about her. Don't even know how old she is — sixteen? Eighteen? *That* old?

These are my things now. I'm on. That belt whisks them by so fast.

I'm standing here hat in hand, head in hat, so to speak. Does she *see* me at all? Oh, come on. White light, eh? Look at you: your hair is white, you are all white, washed out — that's what her eyes say. It's all in my mind.

Eyes on the fellow who weighs the fruit, I've seen her. Probably adds it up all wrong but I never check. She isn't really pretty but her nose is pert, her hair shines, some red lights in it, and her mouth is small — bee-sting, they call it? Freckles will darken in a couple of years, she won't age well . . .

It all goes by so fast.

Making change, her fingertips nibble my palm. She says, I think she says, "Are you sad?"

"What?"

"*Double sack?*" she repeats. "Ess. Ay. See. Kay."

"Yes," I say. "Sure. Don't you always?" Why bother to ask? And then the words rush, just stumble out — "Speak up! Don't swallow words!"

She mumbles again. On purpose, I think. She doesn't look me in the eye now, but someplace below — second, third shirt-button down.

"What's that you say?"

She shouts at me: *"Have a nice day!"*

"I'm not deaf — you don't need to yell!" Going out the door, I'm ready to weep. Now this just can't go on.

The girl is nothing, nothing to me.

Out in the air, I catch my breath. I'm better. I've got to get out more, got to get away. Tomorrow it's the doctor in Bangor. Good — I'll make it count, spend some time on the town. Haven't done that in a dog's age.

If I don't watch it, I'm going to end up writing that girl a letter.

But I won't. I haven't come that far. I *won't*. And if I did, I'd never go near Mullins' place again. I'm not raving yet. But I am shaking. My hand shakes so — why?

I'm famished, that's all. Just hunger, but so sudden strong I feel hollowed out. I have to put down the bag — bags or sacks, or whatever I'm carrying two of. Feel like I might topple over if I don't. I take out the packet of cupcakes, burst the cellophane, dig in with all five fingers. Eat one standing right where I am. Middle of the sidewalk, as it happens. Can't taste anything — only lumps. Must be mumbling to myself again; this lady gives me the glance over her shoulder as she goes by. People can stop and stare if they want, if they've nothing better to do, I haven't a shred of pride. Not a speck left. I'm still hungry, so I polish off the other cupcake and ball up the empty cellophane into the bag.

That's better.

Bench

They are perched there like a row of gray birds on a wire. Birds are friendlier, though — none of these are gabbing.

This is my usual run. I don't like the looks of any of them. Seems they've got no other work to do than sitting like this together, apart. When the weather's bad, they gather at the post office across the street. There's a bench inside, facing the Public Notices, who's Wanted and so on, and they sit and study that.

I'm not as old as the regulars, but my feet always ache round about now, so I've got to take the weight off. I find the nearest bench and set the bags down by my feet. I've got a good view of the statue from here. Always mean to ask who he's of. He's a lot livelier than some of these bench sitters, if the truth be known.

The lady on my right sits and stares. She must be well on in her eighties by the looks of her. I don't know her name, but I've watched her some. When a man glances at her, she fades into the pattern of her dress. Something she has learned to do. She's wearing flowers today, gray ones. Probably thinks they're roses and flaming. Maybe they were once, when the dress was new. She doesn't say a word, just sits there, watching traffic go by. Likes to see things moving, I guess. I guess I do, too.

There's always a knitting bag stashed by her side. No wool in it, far as I can see. She eats her lunch from out of that bag. It's never much of a lunch — some social tea biscuits and a banana, usually. Must be awful dry. Once I offered to bring her a soda and she upped and walked over to another bench. Without a word — like I'd offered her something else on the sly. So I don't offer anything anymore, don't bother, and she lets me sit beside her, quiet, like now. Everybody minding his own business. Suits me.

She's on vacation now. She's worked in her time, I can tell by her hands, they're so rough and burled. Done her bit in her time and now can afford to sit by, hands flat in her lap, fingers spread, face cup to the sun. The light is harsh on old skin. But the warm soothes, spreads like a salve.

There are three men on the bench across from us. "Nodding acquaintances," I guess I could call them, though we rarely bother. Today I do nod, but nobody answers, nobody looks up. Two are staring, another hides behind his newspaper. I can't see a bit of his face, he's covered front and side, but I know he's in there, rustling and breathing small.

I sit and stare at what passes.

The sun is high in the sky. Everybody's busy, cars and motorbikes scooting past; even the birds have their errands, seem to be hurrying. The man across from me has gotten up, he's standing, the newspaper drops to his feet. "You're forgetting something." I point. "It's a gift," he says. "It's all yours."

It's all mine, and it's the Boston paper. Already open to the obituary page, so I scan that first, just checking. Important people, not so important. Nobody I know.

Well, and what's going on today? Plenty. Lawsuits, a shooting, election forecasts, a shooting, another bomb sale. Squirreling away bombs under every green tree, we are, they are. Another revolution, a new one. The same. I'm surprised to see everybody still at it. Where does it come from, I wonder, all that energy?

TERRORISTS HOLD RELIC FOR 3 MILLION RANSOM — that's the big story today. "Bone of saint . . ." Big photo of the three of them. Three terrorists sitting on a couch, wearing paper bags over their faces. Can't see anything but feet, hands, crotches. Look pretty foolish, if you ask me.

I can tell they aren't office workers by their hands. They could be mechanics. Or shoemakers, maybe. Two of them have on those narrow pointy shoes that look so fancy, the kind that's so killing on the toes; the third one's barefoot.

So what else is new? Some governor, name of Laverne — governor of someplace or other, kissing wife for camera. Victory kiss, blooey lips. Well, but they have to, it seals the vote. And there's one of those Asiatics coming off a plane and waving. Head of state . . . What state is it? One of those they've just cooked up, don't ask me. Can't focus: never mind. Paper's flapping too much. Can't even make out what it is he's waving at. Faces in a crowd, I suppose, but it might be leaves in a hedge — that's how faces look in a crowd.

Quite a breeze. I fold the first section away, tuck it under my thigh. One of the maples is reddening already, the first I've seen. People keep on going by. Where they all off to in such a tear?

A bike with no fenders races the light and just makes it. That's it: everything else is stalled at the crossing. Young couple standing there, staring at the red light. Can't hear what the boy's saying but I know he's fuming, feet can't wait, he makes swift little kicks at the curb, marking time. Running shoes — blue ones with white stripes. There's a girl at his side. Nice. Our heads turn.

They do not look our way.

Now they're gone, but I still see them. Standing at the

crossing, just as they were. They're a picture of something, one of those little picture-postcards of the mind. *Youth — the oldest thing in the world*. She — smiling up at the young man, eyes full of him. The girl's hair is long, sunny. The young man is tall. He's staring off at the light, can't wait a fraction of a minute. Her head comes under his arm.

I open up the Living section — it's crowded with news. ACID RAIN FALLS... I've heard of that. My eyes don't linger, don't fix on anything. But they won't stop, either, now I'm started. Why am I doing this? Come up here where the air is clean, the water's clean — and look at me! It's a drug, a poison.

UNIVERSE MAY BE COLLAPSING. Oh, my. "On the other hand..." That's hardly better. "It's the year of the quiet sun." How's that? Sunspots, oh, I see. Live and learn. SCIENTISTS ON THE VERGE OF INCREDIBLE. Sure doesn't look incredible, this little white mouse smiling for his picture. What's the story? Teeth? Teeth of what? I can't swallow this — here's somebody, paper says he is, "growing teeth of chicken in mouth of mouse." My foot! You can't believe a word you read, not one word. "Food of future made from fungus ... tastes like ham and eggs." Well, maybe. And how about roast beef? From seaweed? Or nobody around to remember then? Won't be anything lost if nobody remembers. "Scientists stress superior adaptivity of the roach, make it a fine candidate for space venture." I'll buy that. Always thought those little buggers had a lot of sense. "NASA considering..." Hardier than we are. CANCER WATCH — where am I? My eye must've skipped. HINDU GODDESS RETIRING AT AGE 13. "The onset of" — no, no, let me guess. Wait. CALIFORNIA ABOUT TO FOLD INTO THE SEA. And high time, too.

Take a wrecking ball to it!

Where am I?

Needs time for all of it to sink in. GLOBAL REPORT: IN THE YEAR 2000... I wish them well. Can't focus, it's all a blur. I wish them all well. Me, I'm just passing through.

But wait a minute —

Get a look at this! It's Tito, he's important, I recognize the name. I know that face. He's in sickbed, looks pretty sick to me — looks like death warmed over, as a matter of fact — and they've got him slap up against this girl. This girl I never saw the likes of, in the near-to-altogether. She's in harness, it's an ad for that — full size, it says, satin. Warner makes them. Tito looks away, the girl winks at me: pert. One eye, two full cups, angled just so.

"Anything special today?"

I turn the page, glance up. "Nothing. The same." It's a fellow in a billed cap, come to sit by my left side. Only know him by sight, but I know he's a talker.

"That's why I don't bother," he says. "It's always the same." I keep my eye (still a bit swimmy) on the page I'm now at, my finger on the column (it's about stocks). "Stock prices in New York drop sharply while gold futures soar." But it's no use.

He's going on and on. "You're from away, aren't you?" he says. "How can you tell?" I ask. "Everybody's cousins here," he explains, "or almost. Been going around so long together. That's how I know." We introduce ourselves: Sawyer's his name, Dick Sawyer; he starts right in, talking about this and that. No use, I fold the paper up. And it's a relief, really. The statue now, he's telling me how it's of Governor Bristol, a local boy. "He's sculpted pretty good, don't you think? That rumpled stocking, it's real lifelike. Hard to believe it's stone."

So we get acquainted. He's a house builder. Was. And seventy-two now, worked right up to a year ago. Can't get the hang of retirement, of having nothing to do, nothing he *has* to do. So he's keeping onto the old schedule, still up at first light. He asks about me, my jobs. I tell him. "Tucked away some?" he asks.

"Some."

"Ought to travel, then," he says. "Anybody can afford to ought."

I tell him I'm not inclined that way.

"Only live once, you know," he says. "Now if I could do it again —"

"Oh, I wouldn't," I say.

"Take my sister Em, now. She had a pile of money after her husband died. He was a dentist, and you know how well they do. Em, she's a sharp gel, but no common sense at all. Never did have. Send her out for milk, she comes back with a loaf of bread. So what do you think she does with all that money?"

How can I tell? He wants me to guess, but I'm no mind reader. I smile, shrug.

"Made a lot of phony friends, that's what. Jehovah's Witness, you know. You aren't one of them, are you?" I shake my head. "No disrespect — but they *used* her, you know? That's a sin in anybody's book, don't care who it is. They got her to build a Kingdom Hall, her money shrinking down. After it was over and she knew, I say to her like I say to you, 'Why don't you travel, Em? You still got something left.' Know what she says to me? Says 'I don't want to. All I want is a new kitchen.' A *kitchen*! With nobody to cook for and couldn't cook bannock when she had. 'A new kitchen,' she says, 'and to set on the porch!'"

Which, I don't mention, is more or less what we're doing now.

Time to get cracking. "Time sure flies," I say. "Ha," he says. I get to my feet, shake the stiffness out. "Sure you don't want this?" I offer him the newspaper, battered as it is.

"Well, I might after all," he reaches out a hand. "If you're going to chuck it."

"Be seeing you."

"Take it easy," he says. "Easy does it."

Any easier, I think, and they'll be putting me to bed with a shovel. I suppose I really ought to go places, take a look at the world. I'm comfortable enough, far as money goes, everything paid for. I'm fortunate in that, with so many others living short. But I haven't got any itch for travel, it needs an itch. What they call a wanderlust. I don't have it. All I can think of is the bother — hotel bookings, lugging things, people jabbering away, making no sense at all. I moved around plenty when Dad was young, army brat, lost all taste for it, if I ever had. Lived all over the map: went from base to base — Burma, Japan, Malaysia. I forget. All over. Never two years in the same post. I lost all my pals that way, I always wanted to stay put. Funny how I never did. But here at last I thought —

At Home

The little clock on the mantel is going *get, get, get* . . . Soon as I open the door, I hear it. First thing I do is drown out the clock, just plunk the groceries down and turn up the radio, doesn't matter who's on.

In the kitchen, everything's going adrift. Breadbox gaping, napkins blown. Helen would have my head. The breakfast dishes are still sitting in the sink, growing mossy in the meantime. There are dead flies everywhere, on the counter, on the window ledges; and a few I take for dead that turn out to be living still, they're so slow and dazed. Won't be long.

Once I've tidied some, I sit at the table, my chin propped up on my elbows, head too heavy to lift, and let the song from the radio wash over me. It's full of those "forevers" and "evers" I keep on hearing everywhere. Lies. I stare at the blue milk glass. I catch most of the words, but can't make out their sense at all. Doesn't matter: it's all lies. There's a brown track down the far wall where lightning struck once. That would be three summers back. Or was it four? Helen would remember.

It's one of those times when the hair on my head hurts me.

I never sit in the other chair, the one covered with chintz, but sometimes I turn to it, forgetting for a minute, and ask: "You catch the weather for tomorrow?" Or maybe: "Was that a five-minute icing?" We were happy. As happy as any.

I glance around like I'm looking the place over for the first time, and it's a nice kitchen, if I do say so. I put up the pegboard and Helen scoured and hung the pots. Their copper bottoms still shine. I don't really cook. Sometimes I fry up a little haddock or some hamburger and onion in the iron skillet, or hot up a can of soup in the little aluminum pot that's too battered to hang. Or some Swanson's Hungryman TV dinner that goes right from the freezer to the oven — all you have to do is peel back the foil. Not anything anybody would call cooking. So the fine pots just hang there like sculpture on the wall. And they look nice there, they do, I like to look at them. It isn't that.

The man on the radio is signing off. Ending on one of those double-bladed blessings that make you stop and wonder: "May all your dreams come true!" *All* my dreams? Well, now, I —

Who's there?

Think I hear a knock on the door; unlikely, but I jump up anyway and switch off the radio. No, nothing. Of course, nothing. Now that I'm up, though, I step out and stand on the porch a minute.

It's gotten to be quite cool. A few clouds. Some going by, low and fast, the kind they call travelers. They're supposed to mean rain. We could use it, dry as the summer was. The clover's all dried up, I notice, those brown clumps there. I look out, beyond the burnt clover: the view is nice. Jack pines, spruce, oak, granite winding down to the water. Juniper, checkerberry. There's the sea there, straight ahead, just a slip of it, between that oak and that other tree. It's white now, fading. I always liked water. It rests the eyes. A little patch of water, even a puddle, makes space, brings down the sky.

It's quiet.

Last time anybody knocked was . . . let's see . . . must have been over a month ago. It was still summer, hot — scorching, I remember — rare for here, the whole island was buzzing. People swimming in the ocean, diving off the rocks, that's something I don't often see up this way. He came to the door. A young man with a wispy beard. Eyeglasses. Looks real smart, I think. Carrying a notebook and pen and what not. Census is my first thought. He's got a tape recorder over one shoulder, camera over the other, the two straps X-ing it across his chest. He eases into it, whatever it is he's after, asks some questions about the tide. I tell him it's a twelve-foot tide along this stretch of coast. Twelve or thereabout. I think that's right. "I'll pay you for any old stories you can remember," he says. Told him I don't know any stories. "Oh, I bet you do," he says, "living up here. You all do. Sea stories. And songs — 'chanties,' you call them?" I had to laugh a little at that. None of those, I say. Here he thought I was an old salt, when I never had anything but a rowboat — wasn't bigger than a teacup. A rowboat, and an old thing rutting in mud, this old dinghy sitting in the woods out back. Been beached for years and years. It's leaky as a basket now, full of weeds and leatherleaf. "Any old songs, any old stories," he says. "I want to gather it all in while you people are still around to remember it." Sorry to disappoint, but no chanties, I tell him. I'm not from here — can't he tell? I try to explain how I worked for the phone company most of my life, New England Tel and Tel, how accounting's my end of it, and how I lived up and down the coast but only came to live here at the last. "Don't know any sea stories," I say for the tenth time. "But I *do* know a thing or two."

I could see he was disappointed, so I sent him down to the town dock to try his luck there. Not much, I expect. Fact is, those that know aren't talkers; those that talk don't know.

Never heard from him again, nor heard tell of him. He admired the view, then was off. Everybody always admires the view. Like that widow lady, Lil Whatsisface . . . can't think of the last name. Started with an *H* — Higgins? And when was it she came over? Six weeks, seven? Been a while, I'm not sure.

It's quiet, but for the low droning of the rote. I can hear voices in the water, if I listen, if there's nothing else. Sure sounds like voices. It isn't the whine of gulls — I'd recognize that. Isn't breathing. There are shapes to it, it isn't the wind. Don't know what else it could be. So I say "voices" — all rushing together, with always this "shhh," this sound of shushing over them. Trying to remind me of something, I can't help thinking. Can't make out what it is yet, but I'm trying to, I'm listening all the time. Keeping my eye peeled.

The view is nice, yes. Yes, sure, no reason why it shouldn't be: I'm taxed to the hilt for it, waterfront taxes. I'm not *on* the sea, exactly, but nobody else is — nobody owns the land between the tides. I've got some sort of easement on the sea, I guess, if anybody has.

I built this house. Well, *some*. Not entirely. The woman I bought it off of had no man about and just let it run to rack and ruin. I put up this porch, the new fireplace, put in the insulation and made a sort of attic in the crawl space under the roof. It was nothing but a summer cottage when we first rented. Davey was a little thing then. Came back time after time, come summer. We tried other places, but this was always the best. Started on the down payment must be twenty-three years now. For retirement . . . we had it all planned.

The light's starting to go.

There used to be a neighbor on the right. I can see the
edge of Mack's property from here. There's still a fringe of
old blackened tree stumps, all that remains of the fire. The
land's healed up since; it's green now. First came the after-
grass, then the young trees swarming. Must have been a million sprouts of trees at first, little wisps of trees, all putting
out arms and leaves, and hope — like we all do. All hope.
Years after the fire, I'd stand on the porch here and still
catch a whiff of the burning: creosote, and musty. It was
more than a smell, it left silt in the mouth.

It's still empty property, Mack's is: the realtors own it.
They ought to be able to sell it by now — I don't know
what the trouble is. Last time Bob Danzig came by with a
customer was quite a while back, he came by with that lady.
Wonder how that turned out. It must've fizzled, since I
haven't heard. Can't remember her last name, but I know it
wasn't Higgins. Herman maybe... Sounds close. How can
I remember what's close by, if I don't really remember?

She was a little on the big side. Bob wanted to use the
phone and to give me a peep, I guess, at what might be a
neighbor. The lady chatted for a few minutes, long enough
to tell me she was a widow. Her eyes roamed. Looking over
my property, too, also interested (I could tell), though nothing here's for sale. Snooping around, looking *me* over, the
way single women on the prowl do. Perfect setup, I could
hear her thinking; perfect: widower, own house, two bed-
rooms, must be lonesome, two bathrooms, ocean view, lonesome... Didn't like it one bit, the way she looked me over
— with the eyes of a renting agent! Guess she thought it
over, decided not to, I'd have heard otherwise. Place is a little out of the way for a single lady. She left me her number
— Harmon, Lil Harmon. From Bangor. I remember now.
Jotted it down on some little scrap I have around here
somewhere.

Look.

It's getting dark out and chill enough for a little fire. Trees, everything going blue. I can hear the birds settling, snugging down for the night. Neap tide, moon with a nip in it, just short of half, smoke curling up over rooftops I can't see — only in my mind's eye, where supper's on and steaming, little clouds nestling over the lids of the pots.

I stand, look out, see water, see ridges on the water, see nothing. The day shuts down. Someone touches my hand — it's nothing. A leaf maybe, a skip of the wind, a wish —

You are five months gone.

Night

Back in, I lock up. I *live* here. Can't get over it. I stand at the window for a minute in the half dark. There are still some summer moths bumping against the glass. I can hear the rote, a sort of mumbling now. The dark brings it close.

No coffee, I remind myself. I snap on the lights. Open up a can of soup and fetch a slice of apple pie from the fridge. This should do it. The less I eat, the better my chances of sleep — it's a theory I'm testing out.

Nowhere to go after supper. Unless the living room. I could go in there and turn on the news on the television, but I've had my dose of news for the day. I rarely sit in the living room if I can help it, so that leaves the bedroom. Guess I'll just go there.

Wish I could read a little, that would be a help. I'm in the middle of *The Roman Caper*. It's a good mystery, kind I like, but getting up enough interest and energy even to fold back the cover is beyond me. Time was, when I was a great reader, loved it all, *everything* — life came at me that way. I never was a doer or a go-getter, so that's how I got around. With my eyes. Name it, I read it: histories, handbooks — how-to this, how-to that, spy stories, novels. Whodunits. Read 'em all up. And now it's so hard to open a page — why? Nothing holds me. I sit and stare. There's some barrier

I can't push through — my mind, I suppose, what's left of my mind. Nothing speaks to me. So many stories for growing up, and none for growing down. How come?

There's the Good Book, of course, I'm forgetting. Haven't touched that since Helen. Not since the preacher read it out that day. All those psalms, they didn't help. Nothing but words, fine words, too fine to feel. He left a little directory, too, little index, how to look up the right psalm for the right sorrow: in danger, God seems distant, friends fail you and the like. Praise the Lord, they said. Praise what slays you. I went at it hard for two, three days, then quit. Only thing I liked was something I remembered from Kings, not the words so much as what they made me think of: "Behold, there ariseth a little cloud out of the sea, like a man's hand." I liked that one, always have; it doesn't insist on anything, doesn't harp. A little something to look for, I can almost see it — a cloud, or a hand, lifted out, some human hand. Trying to give me a signal maybe, from out there.

Behold.

I undress slowly. Might as well take my time. Friday: I cross the day off the calendar that hangs on the wall. It's not really over yet, but near. I've survived it. I rattle around in the bureau. Helen used to say you could read a man's life from the look of his closet or bureau drawer. It's easy to see how I'm going to seed, way I keep mine, the top drawer full of money, loose bills and change scrambled together. That's my real bank; all I need to do is scratch up a handful before I go into town.

It's not much past eight, the house so quiet.

A little chilly. Enough to put on my flannel pajamas, so I do. Unlace my shoes and let them drop. I stare at the mirror on the dresser, which stares right back, I take up the framed photos I know by heart and look them over for the hundredth time. First, the big one in the white frame. The one standing forward of the rest. It's of all three of us, the family together. That's me, there, in the middle. I'd set the camera on a tripod and run up to join Helen and Davey. Helen's face is clearest: she's smiling, holding up a bunch of glads, glads or some kind of iris — it's hard to tell when it's black and white. Davey's a little clouded; my hand's on his shoulder and he's leaning away. Me, I'm catching my breath, my face in a fuzz; that's because I'm still settling in, and because of Davey — I've just noticed how he's flinched.

This one's from way back: Davey was a towhead then. He comes halfway up along my leg, he's holding on. The smiling picture of Davey by himself is some years later. He's feeling proud; it shows. Just finished building his treehouse and he's clambering up the ladder, looking over his shoulder and waving. Only a few rungs up, but the ground's cropped off so it looks way high up, seems like he's perched on clear air. He's fourteen: all legs. He's waving to somebody who must be standing back of the camera, back of me, a little to the side. Can't think who it could be, but Davey's staring straight at him. I used to tease Davey about that house, I called it an "airhouse." That's what it was for him, a hideaway, a house for dreaming in, a house on long legs for getting away when things began to crowd him down here.

Did a real good job on it. It's still standing, out in back. Only a kid at the time, but he drew up the plans all by himself, picked out the wood, was plenty picky about it, put up a ladder, hauled everything up there, built a working platform. Raised the whole works from floor to roof.

That was some time ago. I have to keep reminding myself how long ago that was, how Davey's a grown man now. I *hear* him — he calls every other Sunday before the rates change — the connection's usually crystal clear, and his voice is gruff, a grown man's voice. But I keep seeing that other boy, the one that's built the treehouse: his voice was just changing.

I keep a night light burning in the hall. For when I have to get up and take a leak. My night vision isn't what it was. I sleep only a little, couple of hours at most, my sleep hasn't been good for a long time. I've tried everything — warm baths to charm the blood away from the brain, picked that up from a book long ago. I keep my collar, waistband, always loose. That was in the book as well. I've tried positions, hunting for the magic one: face up, face down, sleeping in a sidecurl like something waiting to be born. Tried sleeping on Helen's half of the bed. Tried a little something to drink beforehand, lot of little somethings. No help in any of it. I shift like the sea, this side, that side, this side, all night through.

The sheets are frosty. I get up and move the bed away from the wall, which seems to leak the chill. If I passed on tonight, who'd know?

But I'm not going to die, not tonight. That's just the problem: the old blood still churns, enough energy in it to keep my sixty-watt of mind sputtering and glowing all night long. So that's two lights I've got going, not forgetting the one in the hall. No wonder I'm wide awake.

I ball up the second pillow and hug it close, make believe it's a shoulder, nobody's shoulder in particular, only asking that it be a warm one. But the pillow's too light and cool — it doesn't work. I flatten the thing out again and stretch out on my back. Touch myself all over: cold, warm, cold, cold. I'm hot where I shouldn't be. Old man like me.

Long Night

Wish I could sleep. Keep opening my eyes. Hands won't
stay still, keep reaching for something, roaming, no pockets
to stash them. It's windy out, the walls feel thin. I can hear
the rote. Must be near midnight. Don't know how I know,
my watch is on the dresser, but I'm almost sure. Shut my
eyes and faces swim up, some girls, Helen's too, she's young,
smiling or that's waterlight. Gurrulls . . . I'm going down the
light going something singing *blm l'llup plm* the light darker
all around me . . .

fhhh! hrssh . . .

shhulluhffhrsss! Wide awake — and I was almost there!
Something wrong with my ears, coming unplugged, hear
something — *ohhh!* — somebody crying into a bag. *hsh* . . .
Close my eyes, I can still hear him but not so good now, too
blowy, storm breezing up, boats beating home and one a real
small one coming in on bare poles, not a soul aboard. I open
my eyes, shift the covers and — *plsss!* — I'm all clenched up.
Wish I could sleep. If I loosened . . . if I loosened . . . Like a
river think of a river, river will do all your walking for you,
just lie down beside and ease over, easy now.

rushh! hfff . . .

Please ... rush ... help ... it's so clear. Then whispers, sighs ... I'm not sure ... Open my eyes feeling shivery. Heart heavy, and I'm not rested at all. There's something blowing out there, sure. I open my eyes again, close them, clench up, can't loosen it's no use. I rise on my elbows, tip the shade, peek out — nose and one eye. Can't make out much: only some small points of light on the water, black coast. Black coast far as the eye can reach.

Morning

Waiting for first light. It's still windy out there, but slow — sounds like slush running.

Up before six, touch my feet to the floor and already I'm pooped. Maybe I managed a little sleep when I wasn't looking, but it doesn't feel that way. Might have been herding rabbits for hours, way I feel.

A leaf at the kitchen window lifts and greets me, like a hand. Good morning. Morning, all — I cough greeting back. The crumbs spray out, dry as sparks. The coffee isn't hotted up yet; biscuit by itself tastes like sand. Well, but I'm alive at least, the blood goes round. I'm trying to remember that lady's name, the one who thought of buying in next door, I'm afraid of forgetting things. Afraid of remembering too long. I can hear the mail truck coming up the road, the motor idling, then starting up again — there must be something for me. I pour the coffee, then let it sit, rush to the door and down the path, tuck in my shirttails as I go.

Out to the box and it's nothing but scraps. A bill and two handouts. Sears, some coupons, nothing I need. It's not promising much of a day: a few spangles of rain, a wind that only flutters and falls down, it's so tired. Nothing settles.

The leaves seem just snagged there on the prongs of the tree. Me — I'm snagged here, too, I'm not latched on to anything. And nothing to me.

Even the birds seem scattered. A cormorant flies over, wings huffing. I make my way down to the water. The wind chases the foam crosswise up the low stones. The gulls chase the wind.

It's raining on the sea. The rain looks like smoke out there, seems to just hang over the water, never to fall. Ever want a picture of Useless, that's it: rain on the Drink.

It's low tide, slack tide. Most lives go out on the ebb tide, so they say. I can see the high-tide mark where I'm standing here. Seems to be inching up. There's a little pool in the lap of the rock here, never was here before. Tide seems to be creeping in a little closer every day.

There isn't much traffic on the water. I wait to see what passes, and it's sparse: some lobster boats circling round their traps, a smacker on its way south. An outboard, idling, the motor barely ticking over.

Back at the house I sit in the kitchen chair, making out a few bills and then just sitting. Feeling peevish. Up and out of that chair, I say to myself, it will be the death of you. Up and doing. I tell myself what Helen would tell me: you could have plenty company if you weren't so particular.

Doctor's appointment at eleven — thank goodness for that. That forces me out. At a quarter to nine, I ring up Lil Harmon, letting my fingers pick out the numbers, trying not to think about what my hands are up to. She remembers me, Lil does, or says she does; she sounds cheerful and doesn't mention how long it's been and that I haven't called before. I brighten up some while talking to her, enough to invite myself over. And she's gracious about it: "Why, Will," she says, "that'd be a treat. Why sure, that'd be swell — weather's dull, there isn't anything else to do." Soon as I

hang up, I'm crowded with doubts, though. I don't know
the lady one bit. And I'm not a ladies' man, never have been,
so what do I have in mind?

I'm not really thinking. Only as far as getting out, not
much beyond that. Then we'll see. She doesn't know it, what
a plunge I'm taking. I must really be desperate, it's not like
me, I'm no good at gabbing. Only to myself, and that's from
hunger, and that's just lately. Helen was the talker: I
counted on her when we went visiting. Never failed, a steady
yattattatta. The ladies have a gift that way. And here I was
worried sick, courting her, afraid of running out of things to
say. I'd make myself out a list, used to rehearse the list before I'd go out. I never wanted to get hitched; I was sure I
wouldn't have a thing left to say if I did marry. But the
girls were all for it in those days.

Lil . . . Will. It strikes me only now: our names rhyme.
Maybe that's telling me something, maybe it's lucky. Lately,
I'm full of mother wit, magic, little mysteries. Things I'd
scorn if anybody else said. Connections: like, if I wear a
blue jacket, I'll be run down by a blue car; or if I step on a
shadow, I'll break the bone it's the shadow of; or trouble
comes in threes — thoughts of that ilk I'd have scorned
once. I hate lies, but look the other way on wishes. It doesn't
add up, I know. I touch wood often. And I can't help it, I
don't believe any of it, but the thoughts come anyhow. It's
little things like these tell me my mind is getting soft as a
custard.

Time to shave and spruce up. Let's have a smile. So hard
to face that mirror now. Nose and ears look familiar, but
nothing else does. There's some kinship, I see it, to faces I
wore ten, twenty, thirty years ago. A family likeness: I might
be my own uncle.

Call *that* a smile?

Eyes kind of blank today. It's the expression: no expression: wide open, lightless. But I am here behind the eyes. If anyone would call to me.

Lathered up, white as chalk with my white hair, I'm a snowman. Not the smiling kind. Smile, please — say "cheese." "Cheese!" That's not much better. Look a little mauled about the mouth. Slack, there's no hiding it; neck's the place where it tells. Sometimes it doesn't, though. Helen had a good throat, she used to wear those little velvet dog collars to show off how young it was. Lot of good it did her!

Jacket? Make it the blue one. White shirt: no problem. Some things for the better. Like permanent press, that's progress. Necktie? That's the devil. I haven't worn one in ages, swore I wouldn't ever again. Only for funerals and weddings, and I'm not planning on any. But what the hell, it won't choke me. Don't need to button the top button if I wear a tie. See — the knot hides it.

Here I am, back in harness. All ragged out. I may not look much improved, but I feel new to myself. It's been a while.

Depot

The bus is near due. I seem to be the only one here, me and the ticket taker. Talking in his sleep, he seems to me, his eyes closed. He's got the phone to one ear, though, and he's listening. He nods and I hear him say "I see." Half a minute later, he nods and I hear him say "I *see!*" — his eyes shut fast.

I buy myself a Bangor paper and open first to the movie listings. Anything likely? Not that I notice. The G-rated stuff looks as usual. As for the rest... Well, I'm no judge. Can't tell anymore. But they look to be like some I've seen, and that's pretty much. Seems you've got to be young to appreciate it — the excitement, the ear-clobbering music, all that *jumping around,* hurtling through windows — blood, sex, guts, gore — everybody shooting off from six hips apiece! If you aren't fetching a rabbit out of your hat — American flag out of your ear — grenade out of your crotch in the same split second — forget it — it's too slow, nothing's happening. *Sizzling ... shocking ... explosive* — says so right in front of me. Wonder where they'll go from here? They can't keep on topping it and topping it.

Well, but here's something that's not G-rated. I wonder. *Double Beds ...* looks fairly tame from the picture. Those two aren't spring chickens, if you ask me. But nobody *is* asking. I don't know . . . I'm no judge. Maybe there's something Lil wants to see.

Another ad for the new jeans — "The Poured-In Look." Oh dear. Nothing left to imagine anymore. Can't see how anybody breathes in them, but they must, I guess, so many youngsters wearing them. They're going to regret it one of these days, wait and see. Wait till crotch rot sets in. Yes, or gangrene, I wouldn't be surprised. There already was a case of that, I remember reading about it in the Boston paper couple weeks back. A boy sleeping off a couple of beers in a bathtub and somebody had this bright idea about filling it up with water, and so they did, warm water. Sad. Say what you like, it's sad. And he — what did they care? — slept right on through. Wakes up next morning, they couldn't cut those jeans off. They had to cut off his legs. Yes! Both legs.

Everything going to the dogs.

Any news? Let me . . . No, no use starting now. Where's that bus? I'll pick it up later, once I'm aboard.

I'm marking time. I buy a cup of coffee from the machine. I read the timetable. I turn the cup to the light: I read the cup.

> *It's our pleasure to serve you*
> *Sani-glazed to protect flavor*

There's nobody here. The walls are fly specked. No windows: the fans are still, the air all puddled up, waiting for some flutter through the door. It's one of those rooms where the very air seems brown. There's half a cigar swimming in the cuspidor by the lockers.

Not a soul.

The Bangor bus is supposed to come up from Portland; it's almost fifteen minutes behind time. Dead calm here, nothing doing, not a phone, not a spider spinning. I left myself over an hour to spare, but still I can't help fidgeting. I walk up to the ticket window, tap my fingers on the smudged glass.

"Where is it now, do you suppose?" Talking across a barrier, so I raise my voice.

The clerk opens his eyes, tips back his chair. "The bus that comes up from Portland," I remind him. "The Trailways. I'm waiting for that bus. Where do you suppose it is now?"

He looks me over real calm and slow. "Oh . . ." he sighs, ". . . twixt here and there . . ."

Now that I've got a date, I'm in a rush, everything's too slow.

Town

The mist burns off as we move into Bangor. My tie is choking me. I loosen it till it hangs down quite a bit. I'm still in harness, but I can breathe now. I've made an effort anyhow, shown my good intent.

"Make a fist," the nurse says. "We're going to take a little blood. A real fist. Just going to stick you. A little blood — we can spare."

Who's this "we"?

"How are we doing today?" The doctor steps through the door.

Here I am, perched on a high table, cold plastic and steel on the backs of my thighs, I'm wearing this sack that's hardly decent, split down the middle and nothing under, the nurse has just relieved me of my blood, I'm still pressing a piece of cotton to the puncture, holding on for dear life, and he asks me how — how can he ask?

"So-so," I say. "Old."

"Well, Mr. Ross," he says, being all of thirty himself, "we're none of us getting any younger."

He puts his earphones to my chest. There's something strange in the air. Ether? It's violet and chill. Got a bite to it.

It's strange hearing my name called again. Ross . . . I hear

it so little these days. "Now I want you to relax," he says.
Of course, he read it off the appointment list. If his eye
slipped, I'd be Smith or Beal or something. "Relax," he says.
"Breathe in, breathe out..." The metal is icy on my skin.
"Cough, please! Let's have a big one. And now another.
That's it. Again! Good. For the last time, now. Good, good.
That sounds just fine. Ever short of breath?"

"Am right now," I tell him. The cold metal takes my
breath clean away.

"Oh. Any chest pain? Any pain at all?"

"Sometimes. Just this funny little feeling."

"Hurt a little here? ... Or here?" He jabs me up and
down, still listening.

"Not a pain, exactly," I try to explain, "just a feeling. A
gripping."

"I don't hear a thing. We'll take a cardiogram to make
doubly sure."

"My father had a bad heart, you know."

"You sound pretty good to me, for — how old is it now?"

"Sixty-six. Dad died at fifty-three." Funny how thoughts
go: soon as I mention this, I see my father in my mind's
eye. He's in his last age, and a youngster compared to me.
His hair's still black, so I think of him as a young man, a
younger brother, almost. Except that dying gives him the
edge on me.

"Lucky man, you've got a young heart. Now I want you to
lie back again and relax." He pats my stomach, pokes my
groin. "Married?"

I tell him.

"Oh, I *am* sorry," he says. "When was that?"

"Five months yesterday." Comes out sounding like an
anniversary.

"Ah, that's hard. You were married a long time?"

I nod. "Yes," I say, "a long time." Forty years, that's a

lot of years. Been longer married than I ever was a single man.

"How are you getting along? Family nearby?"

"The boy's in Houston."

"Only the one?"

I nod.

"That's hard."

"Got a good job. His own life. I wouldn't want it any other way."

"I see. Any other family?"

I shake my head, no. "Not around. They're scattered here and there."

"You're not from hereabouts, are you?" I shake my head. "Have any hobbies?" None rush to mind. "How about friends?"

"Well, I might. Lady friend. It's something I was meaning to ask you. What can I expect?"

"Expect?" He stumbles at my meaning.

"Shouldn't I be slowing down now?"

"Oh, no. It doesn't work that way. More you do, the more you can do. Does this hurt?" He's pressing down under the ledge of my collarbone where the bones branch. I can feel my blood beating against his fingers — it's a big beat.

"So I should have myself a fling?"

"Well, now . . . Just be sensible. Better safe than sorry. No point starting up with a teen-ager, that would be unrealistic —"

"No danger of that," I say.

"Times have changed, people are more relaxed about these things now." He's tickling the soles of my feet. It makes my toes curl. "You look pretty all right to me," he says. "Full of beans still. And you're feeling well?"

"Huh? No!" I surprise myself by how definite I sound. "No. There's a lot. I can't read anymore, for one thing —"

"Had your eyes checked recently?"

"Isn't in the eyes — my mind wanders. Can't watch television either. My mind goes off. And I'm not sleeping."

"Oh, well, that's nothing unusual. That's very natural at your age. Tell you something: you need less sleep as you grow older. It's in the Bible, you know — 'and he shall rise up at the voice of the bird.' Ecclesiastes. I could give you a little tranquilizer or a mild sedative, if that seems indicated."

"I'm afraid of forgetting things."

"Then better not. I better not give you any drugs for the present. I want you to sit up. Now." I do. He rests his hand on my shoulder, looks me straight in the eye. "Look here," he says, "everybody forgets things. I can never remember telephone numbers, let alone names, so I carry a memo book. Not everything's worth remembering ... I've got a suggestion to make. You go get yourself dressed and come into my office and we'll talk."

It's not that sort of forgetting, I remind myself when he steps out; not small things. It's everything ... like who worked at the desk next to me, where Davey went to school, the names of Helen's nieces (they're my nieces, too). Dad's memory went completely, at the end. He seemed to know me at times, but not my name. "You sure look familiar," he'd say to me, but he didn't recognize Ma at all. "Don't know who that lady is," he told the doctor, pointing to Ma, "but let me tell you she's been awful nice to me." Some mornings, I think it's happening to me. I know it *could* happen to me. It's hard to remember Helen's face sometimes, the exact color of her eyes. Slate, I think, but they changed so much, darkened with her moods. My hands remember nothing. Whole lifetime of hand on hand, not a trace remains. Touch ... it's the darkest sense. Still, her voice hasn't left me yet. I'd know her voice anywhere. If she coughed in a room, I'd know who it was. I'd know it if she sighed.

"So let me get this straight. Tell me again what's bothering you," the doctor says as I come into his study. He's holding his pen at the ready; he doesn't wait for me to settle. There are a lot of forms spread out on his desk.

"The sleeping. The *not* sleeping."

"But I'm telling you. You don't need that much sleep. Take my word for it. A few hours, and the rest just resting." He's eyeing me pretty steady and I know he's looking for something more. "Anything else?"

"Lots. Air's healthy here, but I don't feel healthy. No appetite, no pep in me at all."

"There's nothing wrong with your lungs. Nothing wrong with your heart. Your weight is perfectly normal."

"It's like I'm seasick, airsick. It's hard to explain. Something like airsick, I guess. I'm just spilling out all over the place. It's hard to say. Open a window — I'm likely to sail out of it. I'm not kidding you, I *might*. I'm not rooted down anywhere."

"You feel dizzy sometimes?"

"When did I say that?" How can I explain it? My life, my old age, should be full, heavy. But it's not. It's so light. Nothing adds on to anything — it's all scatters.

"You know something?" The doctor plaits his fingers, then separates them. "You're alone too much, that's half the problem. You're an intelligent man, but also proud —"

"Why 'also proud'?"

"I think you're sticking off by yourself too much. Brooding too much of the time. Too much thinking gets a man down. There's nothing wrong with you. I can't find anything physically wrong. What you need are some new interests that will take you out of yourself. We'll talk about this in just a minute. Let me jot down some of your family history first. So's we don't forget..." He looks up, smiling a little, making light of it, of how we both forget. "Now how about your telling me? About your father, for a start. You mentioned a few things."

"What can I tell you? He was an army man — that what you mean? Career officer, a thirty-year man. Proud of it."

"Died of what was it?"

"Oh, a couple of things. Died at fifty-three. I told you that already?" He nods: I did. "The diabetes came first, then his heart started acting up. They amputated both his legs — that for diabetes? I never got a straight story."

"Your father had a number of medical problems, from what I'm hearing. Hardening of the arteries, I imagine, along with the diabetes. And perhaps other problems as well..."

"After the operation, he made himself this little wagon with roller-skate wheels, very low to the ground. It made him the shortest person around. Before that, he'd always been a tall man. 'Tall men are tall in everything,' he liked to say. He wouldn't have a wheelchair, you know, that might've given him half his height. No, that was too ordinary, too middling. 'Never be second,' he said, 'being second kills.' I remember that a lot..." But I'm straying: the doctor seems to be going over his white coat for spots; he's turning the sleeve this way and that, scratching the cloth.

"People in my family never aged gracefully, as I remember. Trouble is, I don't remember much. I was young, I never paid attention at the time. You know?"

He settles back, makes a tent of his fingers. "And what did your grandfather, on your father's side, die of?"

"That would be a good while back. I don't really know. People died of sniffles in those days. He just 'passed on,' as they say."

"And your grandmother on your father's side?... Your

other grandmother? . . . Your mother's father?" All gone under. Of what I never knew. "Your father died at fifty-three?" He comes back to that. He writes it down, pinching his lip. Fifty-three . . . it isn't good. "And you're sixty-seven?"

"Sixty-six," I correct him, "no need to rush it." He nods at that, too. "I've got a thirteen-year lease," I say. "What did you say?" he glances up, sharp. "I mean a thirteen-year *lead*," I say. "That's better," he smiles. "You're not your father, you know."

"Oh, I know. But it makes me wonder — you know?"

"Look here," he says, "you ought to get out more. I know a lot of people retired, like yourself, and still plenty active. They get together and have a good time. Meet one afternoon a week at the Union Church just around the corner. They've got a lot going — dances, beano, community sings. Handicrafts. Social meals. They put out a little bulletin about it. I've got one here, I think, somewhere . . ." He fumbles in his desk drawer like he's looking for something slippery and small, but I notice he's got a solid stack.

Beano — bingo — whatever they call it, I've seen them. Seen one, seen them all. Just pathetic. Peeked in at them one Wednesday night at the American Legion Hall over by Mullins', saw them sitting there. In rows. Looked like a wax museum at first, cooped up there, sitting so still. Then I could see they were moving a little, their hands dusting the boards, scanning over and down, their heads nodding in rows. Sleeping in rows, they might as well be sleeping —

"Why don't you take a look at this?" He hands me one of the leaflets. *Bangor Golden Age Club.* I make a long arm to get it into focus. HERE WE DRINK A CUP OF COFFEE — NOT ALONE. ". . . Ought to get out of the house: you'll find you have a lot more zip. You ought to be mixing more, mixing with people like yourself."

What he means is — *mixing with my own kind.* He

doesn't quite say it, not in so many words, but I hear him loud and clear. But — since when has my age been my kind? That's something to think about. He's busy filling out the forms, so I stare hard at the leaflet without actually reading it. There's a drawing on the front. It's got one word under it: BEFORE . . . This man sitting alone at the counter. I guess that's a cup of coffee he's got in front of him. And those curlicues over the cup are steam, can't be anything else. Must be hot. He'll have to sit there and wait. To sit there alone while he waits.

He leans, his arms stretch out across the counter like he's lost something on the other side. The place is neat as a pin, cups and plates lined up in stacks. The waitress is standing arms folded, she's leaning against the wall near the door to the kitchen. It's one of those swinging doors with a little window, shape of a diamond, in the middle of it. The waitress stands there, her face turned away. She wears an apron, a crown with a peak, looks like one of those paper crowns. On the counter are sugar jars, a napkin holder, salt and pepper shakers, two hands stretching, the fingers rayed out, reaching — I can't look at him all day.

"I won't," I tell him.

"Won't what?"

"I'm not a joiner," I explain. "Never was."

The doctor looks up, stops writing. He's staring at me.

"Golden age, they call it! What's golden about it? I hate lies."

"You might consider changing a little."

"I'm not joining any singalong!"

"You might be a little less inflexible. That's part of the problem. Think about it." He stands up, puts out his hand. It's time.

"Oh, but doctor. One little thing. It's the problem I told you about. My not sleeping."

"Try napping in the middle of the day. And how about some regular exercise? I don't think we should prescribe anything yet. Don't worry about it. So you *don't* sleep that much — it's not the end of the world. You're doing well enough as is. Drugs bring on their own problems. If I prescribed a little something, you might really start forgetting things. I mean *really*. There are too many doctors around giving out tranquilizers and sedatives as if they were nothing but aspirin. Their patients give *them* headaches, so it's all too easy to quiet them down with some of these new drugs. Doling them out like candy, never mind the consequences. Why should they care? Fancy doctors, charging fifty dollars a visit. There ought to be an investigation — and there will be one of these days, take my word for it. Let's stay clear of drugs for now. Let nature take care of things, she's the best healer. Sleeping pills wouldn't help that dizziness you mentioned."

"I never said I was dizzy."

"Let's wait, all right?"

"See, that's the thing. It's not nothing, what I'm trying to tell you. If I could draw you a graph maybe —"

"Come back if it gets out of hand, of course. I don't expect it to. You just think over what I've been telling you. Call me. Anytime."

I won't.

I take the stairs one by one. I'm fit, a little winded is all. But I'll manage.

I'll get by.

The Happy Crab

I'm as hungry as if I'd earned it. It's a little early for lunch but might as well. And why not a nice place while I'm at it? No need to stint — after all, how often do I come to Bangor? Might as well celebrate my clean bill of health. Pass the time. Lil Harmon most certainly did not invite me to lunch; I'd have remembered that.

It's called The Happy Crab and there's a bright red crab in the window. Wearing a chef's cap and waving all ten arms, a spoon or a fork in every blessed one of them. That's a man-sized crab like I never saw the likes of. Must be plaster. He's smiling, all right, in the middle of his back. Looks kind of cross-eyed. Crab must be their specialty. Sign says SURF AND TURF, looks a little swank. They've got a happy hour starting 6:30, I see. Entertainment, too — The Smoothtones, Sarah Brown and the Hipshakes, Dirty Laundry, Clouds — that's four nights a week. Lots doing. Place looks fancier than I'm used to. Still, why not? A taste of the high life for a change. Something different.

Inside, there's a little waiting alcove, carpeted, with a brass railing. It's empty, except for me coming in and the hostess standing there, fanning herself with a couple of menus. "How many?" she asks.

"How many do I look like?"

"This way. We've got just the place for you." She leads on ahead. Just the place . . . I bet.

I know where she's heading before I see it. Just the place. How many times have I heard this before? "By yourself today?" Yes, and every day. "Follow me." I follow. Right this way — over there. A quiet place. Is it here? Nice and quiet here. Nice and not too bright. In a corner, thank you, tucked away.

"Here we are." Just what I thought.

Now isn't this cozy? It's the tiniest excuse for a table, a tight squeeze for two and — I knew it! — close by the kitchen door. Minute she gives me the menu, she starts to wrap up the other place setting, the one that was facing me. "Leave it, leave it!" I say. She looks at me, looks me right in the eye for the first time: so surprised. She drops the fork. I wasn't supposed to notice.

Why can't they leave it be? I wouldn't use two forks. Or are they trying not to remind me that I'm eating alone? That why they sneak it away?

I order a Bloody and a crab sandwich, coffee and pie. It's a lot, but I need it — I lost some blood today.

Nothing better to do, so I turn over the Golden Age brochure. It's better than staring at the wall. They've got something they call Leisure Clubs, I see. I hate that word — *leisure*. "Our days are full our hands unfolded rich memories new friends new jobs fine crafts new skills . . ." Trivets, they mean. "As Senior Citizens . . ." I must've left the newspaper on the bus; this will teach me a lesson. "As Senior Citizens . . ." I read that already. "Life really begins at seventy." Seventy — I could tell! — they're older than me. We are still in "the Stream of Life." They're older. "Above all, we must be cheerful." They're older than me. "Our hard work was not in vain." Me, I'm just in the teens of old age, if there is such a thing. "We are reaping —"

Think I'll pay a visit to the Necessary. And take my time while I'm at it. It's something to do while I'm waiting.

When the food comes, I take it slow. I dare them to hurry me. At home, eating by myself, I race through: I chuck it down the old gullet, that's all. No ceremony. But here I'm paying, and making a point, I like to think, so I eat good and slow. The place is filling up now: it's a little past noon. I chew *thoroughly*, and pause between swallows. I stare. If they look up at all, they can't avoid me — the pairs, triples, clusters. Their lips fold in, fold out.

I'm old, see. And all alone. Take a good look: this could happen to you. Chances are, it will.

Oh, I'm making quite a point of it! Where's that waitress? Never looks my way, she's always hurrying in and out of the kitchen, hands full. I'm determined to catch her eye. Question is how, short of breaking a plate. I drum my fingers on the table. There! — she caught it. She signals: just a sec. I'll leave the brochure here. I'm pretty sure I've gotten the gist of it.

I overtip — to prove something. Pity, they never catch on.

We're Together

It's only a few blocks away, Lil's place, so I'll walk. There
are leaves underfoot, rusty ones, curled at the tips like
they've touched fire. Reminds me how dry the summer was.
Turning the corner, I catch myself hunched over, the way
I do walking into the wind and the rain. There is no wind,
there is no rain. It's fairly bright out, I notice, once I stop
gazing at my feet and look up. Now listen, Helen, I say, I've
got to get by. If I'd gone first, I wouldn't grudge it to you ...
But I knows she understands. It's Helen who tells me: Pull
yourself together! Stand up straight — snap out of it! She
understands. It's me that's bothered.

Here.

Now what's stopping me?

It's half past. When was it she said? No special time.
Afternoon was all. Harmon: that's her name on the bell.
All I've got to do is start: my mind's set, my foot's on the
stair —

Up, up. On the way, I practice smiles.

"Will!"

She touches my shoulder: "Come on in." Leads the way
with her nose in the air. I'd think she was mighty uppity

if I didn't know better. I do the same, myself. It's only to hold the jawline firm, the neck at a good angle.

She's wearing a sort of gown with gathers, one of those bright at-home robes you see in the magazines. Hair all done up, a soft fringe, brownish still. Her eyelids are blue. Pretty. Frosty blue, to match her dress and the color of her eyes. She spreads her arms and takes both my hands in hers: I don't mind. We step into the parlor.

"Well, isn't this something!" I say, looking it all over. "Place is pretty as a picture. Real nice." I mean it: it's nice. I admire the way the ladies do it — I mean it, no, I do, all the pretty touches, those odds and ends, little glassies, doo-dads, brightening up the tables, the tables themselves shining like glass. All those clever little details you half hardly notice. Cunning as spiders, they are. Those doilies, now . . . see how she's got them for heads and elbows on all the chairs. Casting her nets, her curly webs . . .

Reader's Digest all over, so you can't miss she's a reader.

"Sit right down here, Will." She smooths the sofa for me. "Take a load off your feet." She sits alongside, a little distance off. "Now we can have a nice chat," she says.

Chat? My smile's sticking to my teeth. Now I'm petrified. Find myself staring off at the cold pleats of the radiator. How to begin? Warm enough for you? Cool enough for you? . . . She's smiling, all attentive. Now listen here, Will, I remind myself, all you've got to do is to ease into it. Take it easy, start with whatever's at hand.

"This place is some nice," I begin. Soon as I say it, I realize I've said it before. But that doesn't seem to matter.

"It *is* snug, I will say. Frank left me very well fixed. I'm fortunate in that. He always took such good care of me."

If she starts off with Frank then I suppose I'm supposed to say something about Helen. But I can't bring myself. Not yet, at least. Can't get over the feeling that Helen's

not far off, looking over my shoulder, listening in. She isn't
wishing me ill, she isn't cheering me on, she's just curious.
I know *I* would be.

Can't think what to say next, but Lil's sensitive, she's
trying to help out. She passes over a little bowl of chocolate
nibbles. I should stuff my mouth quickly, but I'm too full.
I put up my hand: "Thanks, no." She pushes over a dish
of nuts. It's got almonds. I pluck one out, thinking "bitter
as almonds." It's not, though; it's milky, even a little sweet.
But enough. She's really bringing out the welcome wagon.
Jams and jellies and hand-stitched quilts next, I wouldn't
be surprised. I put up my hand again. She looks disappointed, so I fish around for a few more almonds, and she
looks happier. I'm on the safe side. Now, for a few seconds,
I don't have to do anything but chew.

"Something to drink?"

"Not now — maybe later."

I must have nodded toward the nuts; she pushes the bowl
forward again: "some more?" But I'm stuffed, and this time
it's really no. "Nothing I can bring you?" she asks. "You
don't like anything here..."

"It's not that I don't like," I say.

"Oh, I know!" — all attuned. "Your health. Cholesterol,
I know. Just a second —"

She's up and off before I can say anything. Comes right
back with a glass in each hand. One's celery, the other's
carrot sticks.

"My, that was quick!"

"I have it all ready because it happens to be what I live
on."

"Oh, I hope not," I say.

"In between other things." She smiles, throws up her
hands. "I'm always dieting. Doesn't do a bit of good. Feast
or famine, that's my way."

"But you're nice and slim now," I protest. "You don't want to waste away!" I pat her shoulder, little pat, friendly. It's a round, solid shoulder. A friendly shoulder.

"Oh, come on!" she laughs. "Me? Wasting away? Fat chance..." It's silvery, her laugh — keekeekee — like a scissors working. I notice she's got three little chins. She looks soft, big, comfortable. Nice that way — why change? She passes me over a carrot stick, helps herself to one; we touch sticks, toasting: "Cheers!"

"Tell me about yourself," she says, "how you're getting along?"

I try. A little. What I can.

"When Frank passed on, it was the same with me," she says. She comes out with it in a rush, so I know it's what she's been waiting for, to remind me that she's alone too. She leans into me. Can't help drawing back a little; it's too sudden, soon; I'm only half-listening. I look at her mouth which is full, pale, her lips unpainted. I ask myself why, why are her eyelids painted when her lips aren't? I wonder whether I'm going to kiss her and, if so, when, and whether I really want to and, if I don't, why I'm here.

She says softly: "We all do..."

All do?

Haven't been paying attention again. Here I am at last, I've been hungering for a heart-to-heart for ever so long and, now I've got it, I'm not hearing a word. "He was a good man, Frank... The best." Frank again. She takes my hand, presses it a little. "We had times. Didn't we have times!"

"Feel that way about Helen, too. Wonderful woman." There! I've said it. First time her name has crossed my lips. Helen. Words are cheap. I don't feel any the better for it, just small, cheap.

No more spouses, please...

I'm feeling numb, tiny, half my size. "I want to be looked

after," I blurt out, "that's what I miss." I'm shocked to hear myself.

"I'm right here beside you, Will..." she says, inching closer. She takes my hand, strokes it. I flinch a little, can't help it. They're all social workers or nurses if you let them. For a second, I think she's going to take my pulse, but no, it's different — she's holding on to my fingers, spreading them, like she's trying to pick out the best of the lot.

"Now, Lil!" I take my fingers back, one by one.

"Me too — I know," she says, moving off a little. "It takes time. Time heals, Will. It does, you'll see. I was so lonely, too."

Was? Then she isn't now?... This takes some thinking over, but there's no time, she's sitting back now, waiting for me to move. We're both just sort of sitting back, waiting. Can't think of anything to say and she's not helping now, so I do move — stretch out my hand into the air, into the space between us — it hovers, a little shaky there, so I steady it on the back of the sofa, accidentally touch her hair. Soft. Don't know why it's such a surprise, such a shock, to me. Hair, that's what hair feels like. It's just hair. I don't know where to roost my hand. Shoulder seems safest, so I put it there. Don't know what to say, don't know any of the rules: nothing about today is like any day that's gone before.

For a man who wants what she thinks I want, I must be leaving some pretty confused tracks. I seem to be talking about — how did I get on to it? — gardening. About *mulching*, of all things! I seem to be asking her questions — when's the best time for it, and — I don't believe what I'm hearing! — how to judge the best brand of peat moss —

"Oh, how should I know?" she says, sitting sort of slumped back now, sort of caved in. She's really quite a looker, considering. Must be somewhere in her sixties. The way she's sitting now: her wide sleeves fall back, arms so round and smooth, neck not bad. Nice collarbones and I suppose the rest is nice, too. "So pretty," I say. "What?" she says. "You are," I say, "your hair." I reach out and run my fingers over it. "Reminds me of someone," I say. "Who?" she asks. "Someone ... I used to know ..." My mind a perfect blank.

She's fooling around with this little gold chain she's wearing. It dips into a dark place where the neckline makes a V. Some little doodad at the end of it. She lets it fall, then fishes it up again — like hauling up a very light anchor. Watching me watching her and smiling a little.

Fast. She's being what we called being "fast" in my day. That was her day, too. Leading me on ... Nice girls didn't. How they all are now, though. Still ... for us it can't be natural.

"What are you driving at, Will?"

"Who's driving?"

"You never finish your sentences, you know that?" She's still dropping and hauling.

"Well ..." I say. I'm not sure how to move. "Really, I'm not. Not much of a gardener."

"There you go again. Unfinished sentence." Dropping and hauling.

Should I tell her how I'm not used to this? How she's got me in a whirl? Bet she knows. Never mind, I'm stumbling on. "What's that you got there?" I say, bold as brass.

"Oh, *where*?" she says, as if she hasn't got the faintest notion.

"That little doodad there, that cute little lavaliere."

"My little charms?"

"Lemme see." We lean together, our heads almost touching. I can see down the front of her dress, into the dark cleft there. "Nice," I say. It's this tiny tennis racquet with gold mesh for strings. Little pearl for a tennis ball stuck in the middle of it. "Tennis, anyone?" I call. Feeling silly, I let it dangle halfway down, then haul it up again. Be your age, a small voice calls. But why?

"Hey, that tickles..." She giggles a little. I giggle, too, sillier and sillier, don't know what else to do. No fool like an old fool. Feel like I'm in some movie I've seen maybe two or three times but can't remember the name of. I twiddle the racquet slowly, aiming it into the cleft. "Here goes!" I call, feeling all of five years old.

Never done anything like this before.

Of course, I've been tempted. Who hasn't? But I never got up the nerve to do anything. Most I ever did was to write a girl a letter once. And me, married fifteen years! Didn't even dare write it myself, just found a love letter in a book, it was a novel. Didn't even copy it out — just made a copy in one of those machines — a confession by somebody who loved somebody who didn't love back — something like that. Coward. Sneakiest thing I ever did. Couldn't even bring myself to sign it. Wonder what she thought when she opened it? Joke, probably. From some joker. And that ended it. From then on out, I avoided her, like she'd done *me* wrong. *Gladys Swallow, where are you now? How's the weather there?* She had freckles, I remember... It was crazy. Never did anything like that before or since —

But this is different, this isn't a bit the same. Keep forgetting: I'm free now. *I am free.* Her breath comes against my neck: it's warm, it's fizzed, it's furred. How far can I go? I'm feeling more than a bit awake, a hard tickle, a sort of flash below the belt, but nothing at all above the neck. It's the tail wagging the dog, I'm afraid.

So now what? Where do we go from here? I wait. Then she says: "Let's." Stretches forward a little. I stretch too, our lips touch. Tell you what: what? What? Hers feel soft and full, mine — thin, grudging, prim. Hard to flex. We touch, kiss again, linger, kiss again, like we're blotting something that won't dry. Help. I cross, uncross my legs: ticklish. I've got a hard itch, I'm warming, I've got a hard-on coming on and I'm scared, scared stiff. Help me. Got to slow down if I whistle in my mind if I count backwards from a hundred I'll be in firm control if I can remember how it goes... Ninety-nine, ninety-eight, nine, nine, ninety-eight, ninety, nine — where *is* my mind?

"Come on," she's rising to her feet, "you'll tire yourself."

"Well, I." My voice squeezed. "Oh, *let's*," she says. We stand, none too steady. Our bodies sway together. "Got the wobbles, I got," I pat her on the back, on the buttocks, little pats: now, now, no harm, no harm... But it's going to be messy, it is, I know it.

"Come on," she says, husky-voiced, and we stagger into the bedroom, arm and arm. She pulls the shades. I perch on the edge of the bed — there's nowhere else. How far can I go? A little smooching, necking, and then? Let the lady lead the way, just go easy. Remember bundling boards? She must.

The room is small, and close. Something like smoked roses in the air.

"Oh my, this is tootoo —"

"What?" she asks. She's giving off this thick white pollen. Flour? Talcum! — that must be it. Soon as I name it to myself, the sneezes begin. "Bless you," she says. "Too too what? You were saying?"

"Tooff —" I start to explain, but once I'm started it's a jamboree.

"Bless you," she says again. "Want a tissue? There's a whole box on the little table there. Right there beside you."

I help myself to one. "Save it," I whisper. "Enough blesses. You'll use them up. I'm not done yet."

Better now. If I keep my breathing shallow, I'll get by, I think. Problem is, sneezing seems to have nipped that *other* thing —

Well, we'll see. It comes and goes.

She's peeling down so, what the hell, I do, too. I hang my jacket, shirt, and tie over the bedpost. My my, I can't get over how times have changed! Off with my shoes. Way it's done now, I tell myself, trying to get the hang of it. Time marches on. Got to keep in step. Off with my undershirt. This *is* fast — I'm keeping pace, but I'm giddy with it. I empty my pockets of change and spill it into my shoe. My nose is prickling. I loosen my belt, stretch out. Heart racing, but somehow I'm fading out, losing interest with every beat. It can't be this easy. It can't be. I know she's near undressed now from the sound of her, but I can't look, I'm too embarrassed. It's hard to keep my mind from getting up and walking away.

"Anything wrong?" she asks.

Now I've got to turn to face her. She's lying stretched out there, her arms crossed under her head. Nothing but panties on. She must've powdered her shoulders, and her whoosies (wouldn't be surprised). Hell's bells! She's gone and pollinated everything — pillow, sheets, the whole works! Casting spells, I bet. They sell little how-to books on it at the IGA. Bring a potion home to hubby with the rest of the groceries. "Hi," she says, low to my ear, "hello there..." and pulls me down, down against her. Ah, well. That's not too bad. Not bad: she probably poured some potion in me when I wasn't looking, kissed it in maybe. Something she stirred in with a cat's whisker. Or sprinkled pepper in my hair, could be. Hocus pocus, that old Arepo Lemel Molas business. Goes back to the old Eve, oldest hokum in the world. "You're not too tired, are you?" she asks. "Who, *me?*" I say, "this is just what the doctor ordered." Well, isn't it? "How's this?" she says, and I feel her settle over me, soft and warm. Where was I? I've stopped sneezing, but my nose is numb, throat full of this fine silt. When she moves her arms, little puffs or sighs come along. We could do this in the bathtub, now... Wouldn't that be nice? A nice rinse-off before and after. Or *could* we? I'm not all that limber anymore. But my nose is quiet, I'm breathing; if I don't think about it, I'll manage. I'll pick up some antihistamines at the drugstore near the depot. Whatchacallums? CONTACTS? Make me a little sleepy but that's fine I'm not driving I can drowse on the bus back, I could drowse now. She has long bones and they're padded well, nice and round and smooth and full. I could sleep now, I really could.

We're sort of mashed together and it's nice and friendly warm compresses all over and I'm sort of interested though not as much as before. It's wonderfully comfortable the nicest couch ever... couch over and under... A little nap would be just the thing, if she'd only let me.

But she's not letting me, she's all intent. And wearing nothing but skin now. Skin, and a little shag — a grassy patch. How did this happen? Funny... how I didn't notice when. She's humid, the powder's all wore off. I put my fingers in that place I know is there, it's slick and deep and warm, she's concentrating, eyes half-shut and latched very close-in like she's threading a needle. I'm slathering away with two fingers. Three now. She makes a little moan, goes limp. I'm kind of limp, myself. Dismasted, actually. Wonder if she knows?

She knows.

"Does it hurt if I touch you there?" she asks.

"Yes," I say. "No," I say. "I forget. What?"

"Does it hurt?"

"Very much," I say, half out of my mind, so big, so keen

it is. "Would you? Do you mind?" Soul of service. Thank you, thank you, this is very nice. You curly bitch. Where is my *mind*? Pointblank, I keep thinking, keep thinking of the expression what it means. Pointblank... Means: oh wow. Wait — ah — that's good... good, that's even, ah... that's ...*awful*... *Oh, say —*

Son of a gun.

Split. That's it: the end. Spent. All of it. This small, sharp rasp of pleasure, like retching up a straw. A straw — so small it is. She wraps it up in a tissue. One tissue. So small I could weep. If I *could* weep... That seems to be gone, too.

She turns over and we dry off in the air. Stretch out side by side. My left arm, the one under her neck, will soon go dead, it's near insensible now. She's strangely quiet. I really should say something, but don't know what, don't know what the words are when you do it (the first time) with someone you don't know well. Don't want to botch it, so it's better to say nothing at all. A friendly hug maybe, that says it as well as anything. And now to free my wooden arm. That's better: I give her a smile, let my eyelids drop. I'm thinking of — of all things! — soup, hot soup. Or cup of tea. I'm a little chilled.

"Will?" Way she says it, I open one eye quick.

"Yes?"

"I guess we have things to talk over. After this."

This? Got to get up. Only thing I can think of, coward that I am, is taking a leak. "Got to visit the Necessary first," I say. "The what?" she asks. "Oh, I get it." She points: the door's facing my side of the bed. "I'll rustle us up a couple of drinks," she says, sitting up and reaching for some scrap of clothing. "What'll it be? Vodka? V-8?"

"No — tell you what," I decide. "I'm taking you out for tea."

It's a lovely bathroom. I knew it would be. Towels all

fluffed up, all greens and blues to match the tiles. And her eyes, don't forget her eyes! Tiles, tub just gleaming. Mirror glitters like a crystal — avoid it. Womanly touch all over: lovely, lovely. The lid of the can is closed and wears a fluffy blue cover, like it might be a parlor chair. Soap in a china dish, tiny colored lumps of soap, look like little pats of butter, bonbons, anything but soap. Place smells like a pickled garden. Incense? Must be one of those floral sprays.

The room's too fancy, too ashamed of itself; it's a bathroom trying not to be a bathroom, and I'm a man in need, afraid to take a piss. It isn't fair. I think I can hear her listening out there, too. That doesn't help. It's going to be a long time coming in this fine blue and green room with the shining walls. Everything here is something else — pretty, prettier than it is. I hate lies.

On the way out, I'm more forgiving. How can I blame her? She tries so hard. And who needs the truth every minute? Not me.

Gabbing

It's not the same place, of course. But even so — what a difference from before! I'm not by myself now. "For two?" the hostess is smiling. Smiling and beckoning to us.

"For two," I say. We are shown to a table near the center of the room. We sit under the main lamp where the air stirs. The light is big, friendly, gives a shine to the plates. The waitress brings water glasses. She's smiling, too: a pair, a couple — yes, that's all right, then . . . And the fact is, I feel more comfortable sitting, breathing, taking up space. Feel more entitled to it now. It shouldn't be, but so it is.

Lil smiles at me. Once we're done talking menu, though, we're stalled. "How are you feeling?" she asks. "Nicely," I say. "How about you?" She says fine, perfectly fine, and asks me what I'm thinking about. "Me?" I say, "who says I'm thinking?" She smiles again: "You're a deep one, Will . . ." Don't know how long we can keep it up this way. There's nothing between us that goes back beyond a couple of hours ago, and we both know it.

"It's incredible wonderful," she says, after a space. "Our meeting up again like this . . . such a nice surprise."

"Ah, well," it's my turn. "You've been real nice, just as nice as nice can be. I'm very fond of you." What else can I say? I'm making it up as I go along. And where's the harm? She's been making me happy, I'm making her happy.

But she turns on me this foxy look: "How fond?"

"Well, now . . . you want me to measure? Inches, pounds, or what? You want it down to the last decimal?" I smile, but she doesn't smile back. "These things can't be measured," I say, trying to smooth it. "You know *that* . " Appealing to her finer feelings seems to help a little. She nods.

There's a Cousins' Club, or the like, meeting at the long table next to ours. Somebody's having a birthday, and I'm thankful to him. We stop talking, stop trying to talk, when the cake is brought in; wait and watch while the song is sung, the wish whispered, the candles blown.

Then it's back to us. Fortunately, the eats have come. It's a fancy place and she's sipping fancy tea, something flowery, looks like shredded petals in it. There are tiny cakes on a tray, dainty little things — two bites for two bits. Well, but it's an occasion: I don't grudge her. Don't live like this every day.

Never did care for tea. I'd forgotten why, but I remember now. Tastes pretty much like boiled grass to me, this sour, yellow taste. And no *body* at all, no starch to it — not like a cup of coffee. Still, it's warming.

"I'll tell your fortune when you're done," she says.

Something to do, so I gulp it down best I can. I try to swallow without tasting. She tells me to take the handle in my left hand and to twirl the cup to the left of that — two, three times — stop. Enough. Now what? Now turn it upside down, now turn it right side up, now hand it over. I hand it over. I notice a long smudge near the handle.

She studies it. "Looks to me," she says, "like an arrow, or a branch without leaves. What do you think?"

"Could be," I say.

"They're both not so hot. Round ones are best. Like acorns — acorns are very lucky. And rings and things."

"Sure isn't round. What are some of the other things? The *long* things."

"Well, dribbles, or peas in a row, mean money — that's

pretty obvious. I'm afraid I don't see any of that. A ladder means traveling. That's not what you've got."

"It's more like a finger. Am I right?"

"Maybe." She doesn't sound convinced. She's in a study now, head over cup. I study the part in her hair, which meanders, lists a little toward the one ear. I can hear her racking her brains. "Wish I could remember what a finger means. I think it depends on what it's pointing at."

"Handle, I think."

"That's not much help. Close to the handle means whatever's going to happen is going to happen soon. Whatever it is."

She's stumped; I haven't a notion; we both peer into the cup. "Maybe it's not a finger at all," she suggests, brightening, "it's wider, you see, at that end." Our heads knock together. "Might be a knife," I tell her, "that mean danger?" She tilts the cup over her way: "No, look at this. See, it's more like a bulb at this end." I can't keep from noticing how she's shaking the cup a little, helping things along. "Maybe a key, or maybe a spoon," she says. "Maybe . . ." I say, "and what might they mean?"

"Oh, they're easy. And lucky. A key means that doors are going to open to you. A spoon means money."

"Money, you say? So — I lost on peas, but win on spoons. That's all right, then."

"You don't believe a word of it, do you?"

"Who knows?" I'm trying to be open-minded. "Who can tell?"

"What is it you want, Will?"

"Want?" I say. "I don't know." Nothing that ever could be. "I don't want anything." I want to want again. Want not to feel. "What's important is to keep very busy, that's what the doctor says."

"Isn't any point keeping busy if you've no heart in it. Is there anything you believe in? Anything at all?"

"Dragons."

"Oh, Will."

"No, I'm serious. They were dinosaurs really, so all those stories about slaying dragons are true. Well, you know, *sort of* true — much as that kind of story ever is. Not so different from those stretchers hunters like to tell. Even now."

"You might have something there. So that's one thing. Anything else?"

"Oh, I don't know . . . Dreams, I guess."

"Think they come true?"

"They don't lie, anyhow. May say things backwards, but they don't lie. I don't know. I don't think they *come* true — they *are* true. There's a difference. Do you see?"

"I guess."

No, she doesn't. She's blinking a mile a minute — I can tell I've lost her. Can't expect her to read my mind. Don't know why I brought it up but, since I did, I'm in for it. "Like, sometimes — you're wide awake — and you see something or somebody, a house maybe. Or a picnic spot. And you recognize it, you know where you are as soon as you see it. If you turn the corner, you know what you'll find. But that's crazy — it can't be. You've never been to that part of the country before. It's your first time, *ever*. You know what I'm talking about?"

"Guess so. But I don't dream like that, I'm not the standing-and-looking type. I'm usually falling, in mine. Manage to catch myself at the very last minute. Or I wake up, just in time."

"But you see what I mean? It's the damndest thing: I ask myself how can I know it before I ever see it, place I've never been to in my whole life? How come I recognize it as the exact same? Must've dreamed it, I guess. So that's a problem. How come my dreams know more than I know, if I cook them up myself?"

"I'm not sure —"

"So supposing I don't cook them up myself? Maybe I don't even own them — nobody does. Say they come to me from outside ..."

"How do you mean?" She squints a little. "Like, where? Where could dreams come from?"

"Out there," I'm struggling. "Yonder," I'm groping for it. She smiles: "The wide *blue* yonder?" She thinks I'm pulling her leg. But I'm trying, really I am, it's gotten beyond me. Catch myself pointing: Lil's staring off at where my finger goes, this couple three tables over with their hands close together; they're passing the salt. "No, no," I say, "not *there!*"

"Well, where *is* it, Will?"

"Not here. Someplace where there isn't any time. Where nothing ever changes."

"Where could that be?"

How did we get started on this? "Noplace," I say. It's my own fault. Better just drop it. "Like, floating around forever?" she asks, still hammering away. I'm sorry I ever brought it up. Never tried to get it into words before, and I can see I've gotten nowhere fast. "Wish I knew," is all I can say. Got to puzzle things out for myself first; this should teach me.

"I guess you dream about your wife?" She gives me this look. "You feel you're in touch? ..."

I could say: "All the time," that would end it. But I don't have the heart. She's too trusting, Lil. It wouldn't be fair. I don't say yes, I don't say no: I don't tell her how I'm not dreaming lately, how I'm not sleeping at all — she'd love to fix that.

"Will? ... You're drifting off, Will."

"Must of. Sorry. What did you want to hear?"

"Sure you're feeling all right?"

"No, fine, I just got distracted, that's all. Couldn't hear

you with all that jabbering over there. It's all right now. We were talking —"

"About dreams, remember?"

"Sure. Don't you wonder? Where they're coming from — what they're trying to say —"

"Sex. They all say sex. That's Freud. The ocean is sex, climbing a mountain is sex, taking a trip, shoes — putting on shoes, taking them off — falling down steps, putting on hats. Dogs, patting a dog — there just isn't anything that doesn't spell s-e-x, backwards, forwards, or scrambled up. You believe *that*?"

"Well, now, I differ from that. I happen to think that patting a dog means patting a dog, and shoes are just what they look like — shoes. But taking a trip — there I —"

"Are you?"

"What?" I don't follow. "Are I what?"

"Staying on here or going somewhere?"

"Why, I'm staying on," I say, surprised. "This is my retirement home. I told you that. We planned it for years. Putting something by. Saved up, worked on the place. Where else would I go? We gave up the apartment in Boston to come here. I've nowhere."

"Well...each to his own," she says. "It's not for me, I can tell you. I plan to leave for Florida pretty soon now." It's a dare, I think. She dabs her lips, dainty, swallows — I can hear it — too large a lump, tries to smile, but it comes out small. "Beginning of the month at the latest. Sooner, maybe. Maybe *very* soon..."

"This *is* news," I say. "Why didn't you say so before?"

She gives me this quizzing look that says: What's it to *you*? Sighs: nobody ever reads me right. I read her. I could make some fuss, but what would be the point? "Well..." I say, a bit breathless.

"I thought you knew. I mentioned it when we first met. That was what decided me against buying up that land next to yours. I knew I couldn't stick it. Never could stick it through winter here by myself. November through April is the pits."

"You're thinking of moving, then?"

"Might be. I don't know where I plan to settle eventually. Ever since Frank retired it's been Maine for summer, Florida for winter. People are friendlier in Florida, you know."

"Haven't we been friendly?" I inquire.

"Friendly? That what you call it — *friendly*?"

Must be a word for what we had, but I don't know it. "Nice," I add, but see at once that's no better. "Look," I say, "didn't mean anything by it. I haven't got much of a way with words — that's why I went into accounting. You know what I mean. What I'm trying to say." There's a big pause, a dead space, so I hurry on. "So you're going away . . . And fall's supposed to be so pretty here. I mean full autumn. The birch turns gold and the maple red. Never saw it, but they say. Must be real nice."

"Think so? It's starting, you can see the colors starting to turn now, but I don't think it's going to be much. The summer was too dry. You just wait till the fog settles in. Things really slow down. Fog comes in and hangs in there, just won't move. You'll see. Or the rain coming down in buckets. Where you are, your place is going to get a lot of salt spray — it'll be a hard winter. Everybody who can afford to will be somewhere else. Florida's much nicer. Ever down there?"

I shake my head, no.

"Lots of retired people there. You don't feel so out of it when there're so many others. So much depends on how you look at yourself. It's different there. Ever think about it?"

"Oh, some," I say. Me and Helen, we gave it all of five minutes' consideration. Florida doesn't draw me at all. All I can think of are those ads — shuffleboards and pink sunsets, ice in tall glasses with the dew on them, how it would feel to be sitting and staring off at some washed-out baby blue. Near dead, I think. That's how I see it in my mind's eye: this long blank beach. Ocean so calm, so dead, there isn't one tuck in it. "I have thought about it," I say, "and it's not my style."

"No?" she says. "It's definitely mine."

So that settles that. I'm relieved, mostly. The waitress hands me the check, face down on a platter. IT'S OUR PLEASURE is printed across the back of it.

While I'm paying, Lil picks out a couple of toothpicks from the bowl alongside the register. "Enjoy!" says the cashier.

I pocket the change without counting it. Lil turns to me, puts out her hand. "They're free, take your pick," she says, smiling hard in case I miss the joke. "Which will it be — plain or minty?" I'm glad to see she's got her spirits back; I choose one of the minty ones. It's in a little paper sleeve that says:

> MINTED TOOTHPICK
> *We Enjoy Preparing Delicious Food*
> *For You*

It's beginning to *get* to me, the love messages on everything — not a word of them to be believed.

I see Lil back to her door and on into the foyer. Then she'll be on her own. "Thanks a million," I say. Quick brush on the cheek now, a feather.

"Bye for now," I say.

"Bye." She lifts her hand.

And then I'm out in the air, free as air. The sky is clear. Already the moon is up. In broad day. The horned, the eaten moon. Me too, I'm near gone. I'm feeling weak as a cat.

Bench

See by my watch it's too early for the bus, so I'll sit for a bit in that little park by Sears. The one near the bridge. It's on my way.

The wind's struck up, the leaves are blowing. The river's nothing more than a trickle here, and muddy at that. But down the hill where it's full, there are killifish, black bass, and alewives in it. I know. In years gone by, I've seen them. Once a summer, the salmon make a run through, and everybody comes out with poles and drop lines, people standing so thick, shoulder to shoulder, they make a fence.

Only one bench here. There may be a few farther up, but I'm winded. I've been sitting off and on for most of the day, yet the sight of that bench looks good to me. I take a good look at who I'm sitting by, though, and edge over far as I can, which isn't far enough. Don't want to be connected with the likes of him. I don't want anybody to think of us in the same breath.

He's guzzling something from a paper bag and I guarantee it's not Fresca. Talking up a storm, too, on and on and on, but not to me. Not to anybody. Sounds like one of those Titus Moody types. "My idea of *nice*, now, is home-fried potatoes," he says to the air. "In rich golden butter...

mmmm . . . rich creamy butter. Eat your heart out." His face is very red. He's talking to the bag with the bottle in it, how it's a free country, and doesn't so much as glance at me. Not a ripple in my direction. I notice he's got cardboard stuffed into the soles of his shoes. A real deadbeat, he is. Looks like an advertisement for what not to be.

Socks dripping down loose around his ankles. They're white. Helen always said that was the first sign of coming down in the world — white socks, the elastic gone.

Lot of bustle all around. People keep hurrying by, most of them toting packages. Today's Saturday: big shopping day, remember. The pigeons keep poking at my shoes: hard luck, there; walking round and round them, necks jiggling like ninety-year-olds. Can't see a solitary crumb anywhere, damned if I know what they're picking up. "Hey, man!" Who? I glance up, sharp. Not me, nothing to do with me. Bunch of kids going past, intent on their own business. Damned if I know what it is.

"Hey, man, you wrote over me, man!"

"Nah . . ."

"Hey, I seen you. Blue spray paint, that's you, man. You better watch it —"

"Fuck you, brother."

"Up yours, mother-" Kid gives a sort of salute, thumb in the air. Mumbles something — something about girl scouts and Fig Newtons, near as I can make out.

They're all of them booing and calling from opposite sides of the bridge now; I can't make sense of the words. It's fairly friendly, I feel, all this "mother-brother" business, even though they're shouting. Sound just like they do in the city. I guess it's the same the world over; kids in Bangor sound just like the kids in Boston, no different. It's the movies, they all see the same.

They go by so fast. Young and in a rush, always. How

they bump and crowd us! They aren't going anywhere but where we've gone already, but they're in this tearing hurry to get there. Right now, I can watch them fairly calmly, but a time will come . . . Come a time when I'll avoid the hours they're out of school; when I see them coming down the street, I'll veer away. The way they walk, they own the earth. Well, they do, but no need to swagger so! Passing them in the street, even now, feels like a collision some-times — too many near-misses to be by accident. I know what they're up to. We're slow, we're clumsy, we clog the way. They're out to break our bones.

And look what's coming this way — They sure have come out of the woodwork. I don't remember seeing any coloreds in Bangor before. Mustn't call them "coloreds," I keep for-getting. They're "blacks" now. How times change! In my day, if I'd called them "blacks," Ma would wash out my mouth with soap for it — they wanted respect as "colored people."

All this waffling back and forth, it scrambles the mind. In one minute, out the next, who can keep track?

They didn't use to look like this. Damned if *they* don't swagger, too! And that hair, all electric, standing up all over the place! All that energy . . . it makes me tired. One of the girls has a little something — a pitchfork, I swear! — standing right up in the middle of her head. She turns to me: "You say something, Mister?" I must've been staring, but I don't think I said anything out loud. I sure hope not — it's true that I talk to myself nearly all the time, but that's inside my head, and it's not me that's talking now, it's the down-and-outer I'm sharing the bench with. Right now, I just hope she lumps us, if I could move over closer to him to make sure she sees us side by side and lumps us, I would. See: two old fools, as harmless as useless . . . But she's already seen us, together and apart, it's too late now.

"You, I said *you*," she says. I look away, don't answer.
Could be deaf for all she knows. She can see for herself
who it is that's talking, how he's blatting out how you don't
have to go to college to be smart, how he laughs, if that's
what those honkings are. "What do you have to go to college for? To learn to drink and cuss?" I just hold my breath;
she can hear him for herself. It's plain as the nose on my
face how he's out of it, his top hamper gone.

She looks us both over, slow — she's only a little girl. Just
stands there, squinting, hands on hips, that little pitchfork
standing up — looks like an exclamation point! — right in
the middle of her head. The way she looks us over, I can
hear her thinking: too useless to live... I hold my breath
and stare down at the pigeons, no fight in me, not a speck.
I don't lift my eyes till she's well over the bridge. And I
breathe easier, I must say, when she's gone by.

"Jesus — he died like a dog," my neighbor says. He's hawk-
ing and spitting now. His chest sounds thick, like a winter
out in the weather might finish him off. Wonder if he's as
stiff as I'm getting to be? He's been sitting even longer. Could
be he doesn't feel anything anymore, he's sitting off in some
sort of dreamy space he's spun out of himself, isn't any bench
under him, isn't any inside or outside, we're none of us here
for him at all. That's how you get to be, alone so long.

Air's just right, little nip to it, not too much. The pigeons
keep on clucking and clustering round my shoes, though I've
nothing for them. I've got a headache, and I'm feeling old,
older than hell. When I turn my hands over in my lap they
look queer, like I'm wearing my flesh inside out. Everybody
has them but it's indecent exposure to show them — bones,
I mean, the truly privates.

Everything looks a little strange from staring too long.

It's about time to head on back. I'm getting a little hungry
but I think I'll wait for home. Go home and chomp on a

bone . . . funny . . . it rhymes. Stop off at the Necessary first. It's a public place, the walls crowded with phone numbers, messages. And where's Kilroy who used to be everywhere? Not a trace.

Standing eye to eye with me, I see:

Hard luck if you're looking here

I walk back slowly: there's no rush. Moon's nice and bright now, and it's still light out. The lamps are on in some of the rooms above the shops; it's a waste of electricity, seems to me. I guess they'll be going on earlier and earlier now. The windows frame little scenes, snapshots, cheery as Christmas cards. How people live: tables, chairs, hands across a table, faces turned to faces.

I pass by like a shadow.

Night

It's the usual: I listen to the slow wheel of things turning, the same old thoughts, the same few spokes tick by, tick by. I can hear the sea steaming up out there, sighs, rumbles, slaps. Then: something else: I could swear I hear voices, just outside. I can't make out any of the words. Somebody laughed, somebody laughing. This dry snicking sound of laughing. A puzzle, since I'm all by myself in the house, all alone, a good two-acre margin on the three sides, and on the fourth — the sea — the rocks sharp, many of them, and no landing. If anyone came up the driveway I would have heard. I've no neighbors at all down this stretch of coast. Yet I hear them — I *heard* them — laughing plain as day. It can't be something I'd imagine. I'm wide awake — I pinch myself — I'm not dreaming.

So I call out — not expecting anything, but just for the hell of it: "Who's there?" What I hear is muffled, far off, closing in —

It's the wind.

The wind blusters up after this. I can hear water knocking about, slamming into stone. A foghorn blares through. But no human voices. On past midnight, I manage a little sleep.

But I wake around two or three, my bladder full. The sound of the rain must've put me in mind of it. The wind and the rain aren't letting up.

Don't want to lose the furry sleepy feeling, so I make my way to the Necessary keeping my eyes closed, one hand on the wall.

Sunday

Hup! —

I enter the steep air.

Wake — gulping — mouth round as the mouth of a jar. A fly could just fly in there.

There's a stitch in my side: I turn over, pull my knees up to my chest. That helps a little. I drink the thin light.

Where was I?

Just a little speeding up of the pulse is all it was. Happens to me all the time. Times I think I'm screaming in my sleep, I'll be screaming my heart out in my dream, but when I asked Helen about it, she'd say I'm only making pips and peeps, bitty sounds, my mouth hardly open.

Awake, I'm tired. Unrested. Might as well get up: I won't fall back now, I know. I cough; throat won't clear. Better if I get up. Only one nostril operational this morning, and the opposite ear. Feel all tufted, overgrown, smothered with hair. Hair clogging up the earwells now, like those old culverts cluttering up with weeds. If I didn't take a blunt scissors to them every few days, they'd be plugged up entirely. That's what comes of not listening, Helen would say, serves you right for not *using* your ears —

— you hear?

Such a long night. Don't know why sleep is so hard for me now. And seems so easy for everybody else. Horses sleep standing up, no problem there; fish sleep with their eyes open. And look at me. It's so simple, I tell myself, and I know it is; sleep is just undressing, easy, just loosening the bands all over. Easy as taking off a hat. It's like taking a long drink, what could be easier? You sip and you sip and you flow into it, you are the drink. But thinking of water doesn't help because, once I get going, some unfriendly things crop up right away. Like — going to sleep is like touching the bottom of Crater Lake, going down, down, down, touching the bottom that's never been found. Thoughts like that aren't helpful. Best thing is not to think at all, but that's sooner said than done.

Mouth so sour. Did I brush my teeth last night? Can't remember, I was pretty peaked by the time I got in. I could go a couple of days without brushing — who'd know the difference? Dentist, that's who. Can't think when I saw him last. It must have been after Helen took sick; everything else looked silly to me. "How do you feel about your teeth?" he asked me. *Feel?* I could see from his face he was dead sober. I was stumped: nobody'd ever asked me anything like that before, not about teeth. "I don't think about them," I told him the truth. "You don't *care* about them," he glared at me. "Don't appreciate them." He sounded sore aggrieved. "Your teeth have been good to you, they're going to last you the rest of your natural life. Isn't that good news?" I guess it was — of course it was, it *is* — but why did it make me feel so down? Depressed the hell out of me, if the truth be known.

My voice must be all clotted. If I still have a voice. Got more exercise with it yesterday than I've had in a month of Sundays. Was that yesterday? Only yesterday? I cough, clear my throat again. Say to the air: "Hello." Too loud. Again: "Good morning." Now it's too soft.

Never the right amount of sound.

Hello? I tip the shade, peer out: the weather is thick, all right. Feels like one of those fallen days. The leaves of the privet hedge are huddled, clumped in the rain. I can see about two yards out. The rain streaks, blues, muddies. It's raining out, Helen, I say, you aren't missing a thing.

My bladder's full.

But standing over the bowl I wait a good long time, and what comes is feeble, a thread, nothing much. It's cloudy, too, what there is of it, not the usual sunny color. Well, but the doctor says I'm fine, so I'm fine, I'm not going to fret about it. I shake off the last drop.

Ten minutes later, I have to take a leak again.

Nerves, probably. The chill. Doctor says I'm fine, so who am I to argue? Cold, nipped to the bare bone with the chill, is all it is. I'll keep on my pajamas. The leg bottoms stick out under my trousers. Looks a little lazy, *is* a bit lazy. But who cares?

Think I'll boil up some eggs. The radio is sputtery this morning, full of static. There's gospel music on — it's Sunday — a preacher preaching. Got a big, tall voice: "If you are a child of God and marry a child of the devil, you can expect trouble from your Father. It's the living truth . . ." I twist the dial: it's weather: travelers' warning, storm advisory. Visibility low. Small-craft warning. Another station blatting out hymns, keep on going. Weather — thanks, I — Minute I turn this off, I'm going to be down, down so low. Weather again, keep moving . . . A chant: ". . . tin tin tin . . . us curls . . ." Must be an ad. Local weather forecast coming up: "Stay tuned . . ." Keep moving. Question: "What plans have you made for feeding the birds this winter?" Who, me? I'm done planning.

Done planning. Done arranging. Now I'll just let happen.
I'm open: let it come ... whatever's coming —

But not this station, no. Keep on moving. More weather,
it's the big news today, the only news. Airports closing down.
Humidity, visibility, wind-chill factor (it isn't really as cold
as I think it is), a chant:

"Doctors *do*?" (Shocked, relieved)

"*Doctors* do!" (Knowing, pleased)

You bet they do. Whatever it is. Suppositories, I suppose;
keep moving ... Now here's different: "Welcome to the
lukewarm ..." Some DJ speaking, and he's not talking about
wind-chill factor, either. Got one of those sleepy-slimy voices
they call "mellow." My coffee's that — lukewarm, I mean.
Bitter, too: I churn and churn the sugar at the bottom. The
DJ's ranting on, he must've forgotten where he is, how we're
all listening. Telling all the world how much he hates Mo-
zart and A.B.C. A.B.C.? He's explaining: it's what kids are
always handing on, one to the other — Already Been Chewed
gum. Learn something every day ... Now he's humming, and
now he's reading off his grocery list — what's up? He's starting to rail at the sound engineer. Song's starting up — in the
middle of his sentence. Something going on there, the DJ
seems to be gone. Probably hauled him off for some rest and
recuperation. The words are a bit queer:

> *"You're so vain.*
> *I bet you think this song is about you.*
> *Don't you? Don't you? Don't you?"*

Me? Look who's talking! That's quite enough, I think.
Yes, that'll do.

With the radio off, it isn't really quiet, though. I can hear
the waves breaking, the old three-beat shuffle. Actually, it's
quite a roar. And the wind's big and blustery. My water
must've boiled up, so much noise I couldn't hear it starting

to wallop. Oh, cripes, I've steamed off all the water in the pot! If I want boiled eggs, I'll have to start all over again from scratch.

Sunday... Well, and what's to do today? When the weather lets up, I'll neaten the gardening shed. Even if it doesn't let up, I'll do it. I'm protected there. Laundromat in the afternoon: I can watch the towels spin round. Everything's shut up tight today, it's the only show going.

And that gives me almost a full schedule. I could round it out with the Sunday papers, funnies and all, but I won't, I haven't done that since I was marking time with Helen. Always hated the Sunday papers, the fat-with-boredom, dead weight of them.

Once I'm done breakfast, I put on my oilskins and go out. It's some weather. The rain falls steadily. Wind's really ripping up, it's loudening. The garden, what's left of the garden, looks all blown to bits.

The ash are still standing, though. Those young ones I planted myself, a few summers back. They're up to my hip now. Giving off their three prongs of shade apiece when the sun is on them, they've still got a ways to go. I never cared for gardening, not for flowers or low shrubs like Helen liked. But a tree — that's different. Don't know why I like these little fellows, they'll never be much in my time. "You know, Will," Helen used to remind me, "you aren't going to be around to talk eye to eye with them." I know that.

I make my way down to the edge. Tide's racing in, the waves crowding one on another. There's some visibility, not much, but more than I thought there'd be. The gulls are heading inland. They know something. Something's coming. Everything's rushing: petrels hurrying over. A couple of oldwives in their span-white caps. The gulls go by, flying low, mewing, hugging the water close. The wind is freshening.

Broody weather: there's something afoot. The tide's coming in, but that's not it. It's something in the speed and shape of the waves, the way they're bent over. They're hurrying and they're crouched. Must be the wind and the rain flattening out their tops —

I walk the jumbled stones, looking over the rubble as I go, the bits of broken — rope, oarweed, a toggle, some boards plated with kelp, seawrack — everywhere scads of it. Devil's-apron, a rusted hinge. Bottle glass, more boards — they look salvageable. Two-by-fours: clean ones, must be planking from the hull of a boat. A fairly large boat.

Not a soul. Standing right here, I don't really mind; it's in the house I feel it. Spot like this, people don't make much of a difference. Hundreds of years ago, this coast must have looked the same: bare bones and a little spruce cover; hundreds of years from now, I expect it will look the same, the water coming and going, the same.

Living Room

Nicest room in the house, but I don't feel at home in it. I'm not going to sit here long. I move from the big wing chair to the sofa. Then from sofa to rocker. I poke at the cold fireplace. Flue open? It is. Pipe for the wind that's blowing; even here the sea comes in. I pace a little, stare out the window a little, pace a little more. Stir up, scatter the dust. Let nothing settle.

I could turn on the television and pick up the early news. *Eyewitness News*, the news with the personal touch: those reporters really get *in* there. Like to stir up the blood. You can hear it — little shakes in the voice — they're excited. Human interest, they call it. "How did you feel when your husband was stabbed, when you heard him call out?" Now close in real close on the lady's face now, that's real good. She's not acting so it's like the finest kind of acting. "Tell me, how did you feel when you saw your baby burning?" Ask again; she's not paying attention.

How do you think it feels? It *feels*.

I'm in a smudge.

Can't rest here at all. I try it out maybe once a month and it's always the same. After today, I don't think I'll come in again. Unless company comes, which isn't likely.

How about if I closed it off? I did that with the small bedroom. And the spare room is only for storage now. I keep them both locked. I could live in my two rooms. Bedroom and kitchen is all I need. Oh, and the Necessary. That's two, two-and-a-half rooms. The rest isn't doing anything. I could rent them, of course: Davey's and the spare, and this where I'm sitting — it would bring in some money.

But I know I won't. I couldn't with Davey's, and this is our best room and it *is* nice. That little table with the paw-pads for feet is a real genuine antique. A most wonderful table. And the highboy over against the wall is almost two hundred years old. Mint condition, just as good as it ever was. That came down through Helen's grandmother. They worked with love in those days, made things to last. Not like now.

Some nice: those old prints on the wall. The red and green ship's lanterns on the mantel, port and starboard in the right places. It's that I can't stand, all that loving detail. She was so proud of this house, she wanted me to have a drawing made from a photograph of it. They do that. I've still got the brochure for it — Holub's his name. Lives over in Westfill. Calls them "house portraits." Would've cost us a small fortune —

Didn't we have plans?

Men are supposed to go first — I'd counted on that. Helen would move up here with one of her widow friends and spend the last of it gardening and canning and putting up jams. It wouldn't be perfect, but she'd be better than me at keeping on. That's a fact: women are.

The room is still, so still, so perfect. I sit on my hands, so as not to muss anything. Got the fidgets, they won't stay sat on for long. There they go — free — hunting for work or mischief, whatever's available.

Something down there, between the cushions, I'll give it

a tug. Green. A scarf. Must be Helen's but I don't recall seeing it before. Can't think how it got there. It's gauzy, shot
through with silver threads. Slithers like water through my
fingers. I toss it away — it spreads in the air — a sail — It's
all so slow. It folds back onto my knee. Clings there, slinky,
silky, caressing. Soft as lint. I lift it by the edge using only
my fingertips, then flick it off. It flutters down, all filmy.
Collapses near the leg of the chair. It's a tease. Can't get my
eyes unstuck from it, and I'm not about to touch it with my
fingers again, so I get up and leave it there. Shut the door
behind me as I go.

Afternoon

For lunch, I open up a can of Franco-American spaghetti. Doesn't taste much different hot or cold, so I eat it cold, right out of the can with my fingers, lifting the strings out in bunches, then fork up some of the mess from the bottom — it's mostly sauce. There we go. No dishes to wash, so I feel clever and thrifty, but when I go to chuck the empty can, I notice I've splattered some of the red on the front of my shirt. Doesn't matter. I'll toss it in the hamper with the rest of the laundry. Have to do the wash today anyhow.

The refrigerator door is standing half open, don't know how long that's been. I open it full and shut it tight, slamming it, testing. There's nothing. Absent-minded, that's all. Tired, I lean my head against the long smooth side, just rest my forehead on the smooth a minute, it rests me. It's got a hum inside, I can hear it, steady, with dips in it, a sort of heartbeat.

If anybody caught me standing here, they'd really wonder —

Things must be quieting outside. From here, it's hard to tell. The rain is letting up, I think, but the fog seems to have settled in. It's warm, though, no excuse for not going about my business.

I've got two sheds standing side by side. One's a lean-to for stacked wood. Slatted sides. I've put in about a cord and a half now — chopped, but not yet split. Splitting's my next job. Come winter, I plan to burn two cords; for the rest — oil. The top logs are damp. First frost, I'll have to store the wood inside. Or fill in the slats maybe on this.

The tool shed alongside is a proper little shack, caulked like a boat, and tight as a barrel, I like to think. Only, somehow, it's damp inside. Close and damp. It's a history of our lives. Here's Davey's old bicycle, and the double-deckered birdhouse I spent so much time putting together, but the birds never took to. All my tools, power cords, some strips of flashing, wad of tarpaper, all Helen's gardening gear — trowels, clippers, pots, peat moss, potting soil, hand rakes and I don't know what-all. Burlap sack full of bulbs. Tulips? I forgot to ask, other things on my mind. She had no time to put anything down this year. Bulbs are supposed to go into the ground long before their season, that's all I know, but I don't know what the season for this batch might be. Her precious seed books are stashed on the one shelf; they're a little damp, too. I'll take them back into the house.

She was the one with the green thumb, Helen was, she could tell the time of day by the flowers, whose head was up and how high, whose down. You have to know to tell, but she could. The weather, too — we had a couple of plants that told the weather before it broke, curled up before the rain came. I forget which ones; they're still around. Someplace. They weren't all that much help really, when it came right down to it, since the rain had to be close and, by then, I knew it, my old bones knew it.

Some plants are really clever, though. Like those night blowers Helen told me about, the ones she showed me the pictures of. This pale, chilly little flower, kind of sickly looking, that gives off scent in puffs from eight in the evening to

midnight. On the dot, every half hour. We don't have any
of those.

Inside, I lay the seed books out on the kitchen table to
dry. *Serenity Farms, Whitemost, The Merry Gardens*, they
all smell a bit mildewed. *Legends for Little Folks* — that's
not seeds. It's quite damp, swelled up; even the cover's rip-
pled. Plenty of pictures, I see... Must have been Davey's.
Short chapters and the print so clear and big, that takes me
way back. When I used to read to him before bedtime.

Wonder whether it's worth saving. The pages are so
bunched together. Here's Father Time, all stooped over.
That's me — I'm getting there. "The Girl Who Turned
Into a Tree"... Now isn't that something! I don't remember her, and she's pretty hard to forget. Looks exactly
like a tree, she's halfway turned, her hair's standing on end.
Her hair's a mess, a real bird's nest. No use combing *that*.
She's in a freeze, I can tell, just wooden with fright, her legs
joined solid. They're shagged or scarred or maybe that's a
long dress sketched in none too well. And her toes! Longest
I ever saw. Her feet sure aren't pretty, spreading out like that,
toes so long and knobby and twisted, starting to root down,
I guess, into the grass.

Here's "The Man in the Moon." I've seen him myself at
the full, this old man bent under a load of sticks. Thought
I saw his wife coming along after him a couple of times. And
a dog, once. Here's another moon story: picture's prettier.
"Young Forever, Loved Forever." Ha. Nice trick, if you
know how. What's the secret? Moonbaths? Lot of moon-
beams plashing about in the picture. Somebody sleeping,
must be a shepherd, he's got this crock — crock or crook,
whatever you call it — and all these little lambs, kind of
sweet, sleeping in a ring around him. Cute, but kind of silly.
He looks pretty smug, too — like he's swallowed the secret.
Kissed to death, probably... By Jesus — here's something to

look at! Picture of this gal with snakes for hair. "Turned to Stone," it's called. Looks like somebody's bad dream to me, though the lady's really not bad looking. Reminds me of Lil, a little. Handsome, but for the hairdo.

Don't remember reading any of this stuff to Davey, but I guess I did. See if I can dry it off. I'll stand it open if it will stand, and fan out the pages — that might do it —

So. What else have I here? *The Catalog of Extra Earlies. Burpees. The Sitting Bulb. The Rambling Gourd . . .* It's quite a spread, I'd forgotten. I'm always surprised afresh. There are so many, so many kinds. Smooth, and fuzzed, and rumpled — bells and cups and purses. Ruffled, bearded, pleated. Spicy, flaming, frosty . . . Dream it, draw it — it's been thought of. It's around here — somewhere — already here and waiting.

Evening

I'm done with the Laundromat. No sooner do I step in the
house than the phone rings. It's Davey.

"Dad, how are you? How you doing?" I say fine, like I
always do. "I haven't heard from you in a long time —
what's new?" he asks. "Me?" I say. "What could be new?"

"How's the weather?" he asks. I ask about his weather.

I ask about Katie, the dogs. Trying to steer clear of all the
subjects we disagree on leaves precious little left over. It's
like walking on eggs, on glass. I ask him how about a Thanks-
giving visit. He tells me he'll see, which means he won't. He
reminds me he only gets the one day off, so I know he won't.
And I don't know how it happens, but before I know it,
we're off, into one of the same old arguments.

"Why are you staying on up there?" he asks. "In the middle of nowhere."

"You really want to hear?"

"I'm asking, aren't I?"

"I told you before: it's what we planned."

"People *change* plans!"

"I don't. I'm staying. This is my home now."

"Summer, I can understand. It's staying on after that
makes no sense. It's not like you were sitting out in the sun
someplace. What are you going to do when winter comes?"

"I'm staying put. My mind's set."

"You have any idea what the winters are like up there?"

"I like to be by the water."

"Why? What's the use of it?"

"No use, that's why I like it. It keeps reminding me."

"What are you talking about? Reminding you of *what*?"

"Never mind, that's my business. Something personal —"

"You aren't making any sense, Dad, know that? You could be in a nice apartment someplace, lots of nice people around. Activities. Things to do. You don't have to be by yourself."

"Sure, I know. Bingo."

"Dad? Are you listening? I'm talking about another house, an apartment, a really nice apartment. Wall-to-wall carpeting. For what that house has cost you, you could buy a condominium. A *condominium* — you realize that?"

"There isn't going to be a next house. Be wall-to-wall soon enough."

"If you had a car at least . . . Why'd you sell the car?"

"What do I need a car for? I'm not going anyplace."

"You're acting like an old man, Dad."

"What do you think I am?" *Who does he think I am?* "I *am* an old man!"

"That's not what I mean — I mean older than you have to be. You're getting to be Mister Old. You know you've been hollering at me? You started right off —"

"I'm not *hollering*! It's the connection — it's no good." I'm telling myself to take a deep breath, count ten. I count up to six, then stop to listen: Davey? No voices now, but it isn't quiet. I can hear the storm, a flat steady blowing — or maybe that's Davey breathing out at the far end. He's waiting for me to say something or hang up. But I'm not ready to say good-by, so, scratching around for something more, I light on the treehouse: Should I have it taken down? It might be a hazard in a storm, but it's Davey's after all, it isn't mine.

"Treehouses are for kids, Dad. I'm not a kid, I'm thirty-six now. You forgetting? *Thirty-six*! It doesn't matter to me what you do with it."

"Maybe your own kids would like to have it one of these days. Ever think of that?"

"I *knew* it! How do we always manage to get on this subject?" He's talking too fast, too loud; I shouldn't mention kids, I should've known better. "I told you before: no kids! I'm not going to have any. We discussed this before, Dad, I told you a million times — Katie feels exactly the same way I do."

"I see."

"Do you?"

"No, I see all right," it's hard keeping my voice level. "I forgot — you have dogs instead —"

We hang up, both at the same minute.

Fighting the Blues

A little respect, that's all!

Getting to be Mister Old, am I? Well? I know him. Know how he walks along, how he shuffles on the threshold of the door. Must've been rehearsing it for years. I know how he looks, the costume: don't care and nobody cares. But where's that mildness he's supposed to put on? Things come at me sharper than ever before. The cold, keener. That wind, now — brother! Feels like it wants to kick in the door.

What *am* I going to do, come winter? Sit in my long-handles and hug the stove? I batten down all the windows, then crumple. I am so pared down, I have so little pride left, with a thumb you could put out my heart. I ring Davey back, and it's as usual: we start to make amends, then start all over again. To top it, the storm must be playing with the wires, the connection's unreliable, our voices fading in and out, strange voices bursting in. Two of them so loud and clear they might be coming from the next room. Somebody says: "Hauled a hundred traps, used brim for bait," and somebody asks: "Still hauling?" and the answer: "Little bit." — I butt in: "Davey?" No answer — a chirring. Then the sound, sounds like somebody gobbling the wires. Then I hear Davey yelling: "How should I know? What kind of question is that?" — I holler: "What question?" — "I told you already," he hollers back, "it's no use." Too much wind and water going to hear a thing. We're both yelling now, with the storm between us.

Give it up.

How to finish off my day? I set myself down in the kitchen, turn up the radio, get a blast of static, work down the row, get nothing but static, switch it off. Then I remember the booklet I bought at the Laundromat. It's in my jacket pocket, just a tiny little thing, clear forgot I had it. Called — what's it called? Blue book? Little blue...? Here, I've got it: *Fighting the Blues*... Picked it out because I'd never seen a book you could buy off a machine before. One of those vending machines that sells aspirin, antacid, nail files, Chap Stick, and the like. Just curious. For two bits you can't lose much, I tell myself. Not with what everything's costing nowadays. Cover's a nice color, this violet-blue. Makes me think of outer space, of how tiny we look from up there. Don't know whether that's consoling or not. I guess not really.

Not much to it. Fits right into the cup of my palm. Short paragraphs, so it shouldn't be hard to keep my mind on it. It's a list, really. Busy work and lots of it: "Clean out... throw out... get rid of... hang a new... open a window ... take up knitting... Ring up... bring up... make a list ... Organize... How the celebrities do it... God is a comfort... alcohol isn't... find a guru...

> *"What you do comes back to you.*
> *Nature's way of telling you..."*

That'll be doing it. And mighty quick — seven minutes, was it, cover to cover? Go back? I must've passed over the magic formula, the one that's tailor-made for me, like maybe let in the sun or take lots of vitamin C. Or E? That for baldness? But no, that's it — enough. I'm done. I think of that psalm, the one of consolation, the one that goes "he keepeth all his bones; not one of them is broken." I notice the lights are dipping. Better set up the storm lantern. And have the flashlight handy — that's under the sink in the kitchen. Stop a second: listen to the wind.

So . . . that's it. Lantern, matches, flashlight, I'm ready. Sunday: it's been a long day; I'll cross it off the calendar before I turn in.

Something clanging out there.

Storm

He comes kneeling, rocking, out of the sea. A horned sea:
fish with hard horned tails knocking against the hull of my
boat. I'm in my little peapod, scared stiff, trying to beat it
to shore. Soon as I hit land, I jump clear of the boat. Start
to run for it — the rain's belting down. Then I turn and
look back at the water. See only a barrel tossing. The boat's
melted away. There's a hoop out there tossing, hoop of a
man, belly upward on a wave. I wait. The waves nudge him
in. A man: kelped, sea-gray, streaming. On his knees. Elbows
out, hands fisted, he comes rocking out of the sea. Water
seeps from his mouth. His face never changes — it's O for
surprise — stony, his mouth a dark hole, and his eyes are
locked open on someone or something behind me I can't see.
Between his thighs, there glistens

a toad

I hear — it seems to be coming from somewhere behind
me — somebody calling. It isn't any voice I know.

It sounds like a toad.

*

A foghorn. The small window in the bathroom must've flown
open. The storm's come into the house. Heaving the win-

dow to, I get a face slap full of the weather. Slap of the
sea — I'm wide open, wide awake. The wind howls, rattles
the glass. The wall is thin. I bury my face in the towel, it
smells brackish. The dream comes back to me. Back into
bed, not expecting to be able to fall off again, but sometime
before sunup I do.

Waking, the first light is nothing much. It brightens very
slowly. I had a dream but it's hard to remember now. Something about a boat. There was a statue. I forget just how it
was. It came back to me when I got up to fix the window.
I had it, but I lost it.

The rain is quieter when I wake for good, only rustling a
little, and I think it's over and done. By the time I sit down
for breakfast, it's started up again. An hour passes till it
slackens off entirely.

Round past nine, I step out to inspect the damage. The
house is all in one piece, telephone wire, chimney, and aerial
still standing, but some of the smaller trees in the yard (one
of the ash I planted) are a bit bowed and bedraggled. A
couple of branches from the big oak are down. Better watch
it where I'm stepping — there are puddles everywhere. The
dogwood bushes look ragged, just shredded. Wonder why
they took it so hard. I've been putting off looking at the treehouse, but today I know I've got to. It could be a public
nuisance; another storm like last night, a loose board or two
flying around — anything happened, I'd be to blame.

Treehouse, Airhouse

There it is — perched up there a good fifty feet in the air —
this lookout atop the tallest tree I own, this broad-branched
pine. Mast pine; it's higher than my hemlocks. How memory laps and laps it round...

The color's weathered out, grayish now, exact same as the
bark. A secret place. Blends so, it's hard to see there's a treehouse up there, unless somebody's tipped you off.

Ladder's in place. *Seems* firm. I shake it a little to test it:
no, it's firm. Haven't been up it in a year or more. Here
goes. Hope I'm steadier than I think I am. I put out my
hand and touch the bark. The trunk is scarred, rossy, but
solid. It's not a young tree; the lower branches are gray and
bearded. Rungs still a little wet and slippery: I'll have to
place each step. Sure looks steep. Alley oop — It's sky above
and sky below, no nets to catch me if I fall.

Lead with the right hand, left foot — there we have it.
Fixed foot, loose foot. That's it — hand, foot, hand, foot,
keep going, keep going, keep up the rhythm now.

Rest a minute a ways up, catch a second wind. I can see
the ocean real well from here: looks cold, whitish, with low
cross ridges. What they call a short sea. Tell myself to take
a few long breaths, suck it in slow. I can see way way out, a

mile maybe or more. There's a lone salt banker threading her way past North Cod, but no other boats about.

I try to look up — it's hard. Can't see much but the underside of the floor from where I'm standing, can't stare too long. Angle cricks my neck. Looks pretty sound, what I can see of it. Left side a little sagged maybe? . . . Maybe. It's hard to say. It isn't like other treehouses I've seen, those boxes and A-frames. Davey did the plans: it's built in the round, started out looking like a wheel, the floorboards sprung out from the trunk like spokes. Shingle roof . . . I can't forget watching Davey — Davey, who never had a bit of patience, soaking those shingles in brown stain, dipping them one by one, making sure they stained all over even. It was *his* house, so he took pains. Took his first girl up there, as I recall.

Better be moving on.

If I rest too long, I'll forget where I am and step off onto air. Clear air. I hum as I go higher, to keep my spirits with me. Thought I felt . . . Nothing.

Something?

Something brushes past me — slight — Thought I saw. Yes. There he is, little thing, near eye level now. This little worm, green, no bigger than a hangnail, floating alongside. Traveler, like me. Dangling from this hair, that's all he's got for hanging onto, this whiskerbreath he's breathed out of himself, he's spooling round, trying to get a fix on something, he's after something, trying to find out what's out there beyond where he's at. Getting me dizzy, can't watch too long. I step up and he drifts down. The long needles scratch as I go by — like kissing a lot of brooms. Careful, I. I can't afford to sneeze. Not now! Wings flap at my coming — I hear them — skitters, shrills of warning from branch to branch, but no bird comes out to see. Clear view of my front yard here. Rusty in patches. Not seeded well. It's easy now, rung after rung. Funny how it's like going deeper, going up but also down, the quiet deepening as I go. I'm nearing the place and a good thing, too. Better not look beyond my hands now, head a wee bit spotty, swimmy, spots of sun I see round keep going round, look at the rung above, hand over hand that's the way, I'm there, nearly — almost there —

Here's the overhang. Door's like a cellar door in reverse — it opens *in*, right up into the floor. I give it a heave and — nothing! Doesn't budge. Holy Christ! Something I should've thought of — *down there!* Think. Better think hard now. Swollen with damp, must be . . . If I had a screwdriver — or a knife — Nothing but bare hands. No help for it: I push again, *mightily*, putting everything I can spare into it — head, shoulders, arm — and, grudgingly, it gives —

Hoist myself up and inside. I'm out of breath. Shaking. Shaking like a leaf. Sit a minute, hunched over, on the first patch of floor, waiting for my heart to slow. My right arm aches clear up to the socket.

Place is full of shadow.

Once I've begun to catch my breath, I push the door back so I don't keep staring down at the drop. Now it's even darker. I move away from the door, looking for a place to resettle. I touch the wall. A thread clings to my hand, spider's silk. I knock over a can. It's a big coffee can, all scabbed over with rust, the kind Davey used to use when he was spending most of the day up here, too lazy to come down and take a leak.

The floor feels pretty steady. Chill, but drier than I expected. Running my hand along the boards, I find bird droppings everywhere. And broken threads — place must be full of cobwebs. "Tents," Davey called them, "spiders' tents." Butterflies were "flutterbys." Seems like just the other day. It's still fresh in my mind.

My eyes are beginning slowly to take hold. Nothing *looks*

loose. Beams, boards, all in place, far as I can tell. I've forgotten what's up here, how this room goes. The light is
small, and the morning was dim to start with. It takes me a
while to learn to see.

When I do — it knocks the wind right out of me. Over in
the corner there: a boy sleeping. Nobody I know.

Scram! Clear out — I tell myself. He's a stranger — up to
who knows what — *Get going!*

And he's here first. Could be on the run from someplace.
In trouble —

Better just scram.

But he's sleeping pretty, his cheek's smooth and rounded,
he's scarcely more than a child. There can't be any harm in
him.

Can't be, I just know. He's not ready to spring, lying so
loose, so still there, sort of smiling to himself. He's not going
to jump anybody. There's an old mattress leaning against
the wall, only a few feet from him, but he's not on it; he's
lying on the bare boards. Sick, is my next thought. But that's
not likely. He doesn't look a bit sick, and he couldn't have
made it up here in one piece if he were feeling the least bit
off.

He can't be more than fourteen — fifteen. Might be even
younger, but I guess not — his Adam's apple sticks out. He's
lying on his side, facing me, been turned that way all along.
Hard to think how I missed him at first now that I know
he's here. He's dark. Not dark, really: tanned, hair's too
bright. Must be gold in the sun. Like summer. That's what
he looks like, like someone left over from summer. There's a
stash of acorns not far from his foot, some squirrel's treasure.
He doesn't stir.

I'll just go over to him. Step gingerly — better yet, crawl;
all I need is one loose board. Wish I knew who the hell he
is, what he's doing here. Close enough. He still doesn't stir.

I'm beginning to wonder whether he's alive or not. I bend my ear low to his mouth. Yes: alive and sleeping sound, breathing calm. Babies sleep like that, and why not? No regrets.

He sure is having himself a fine snooze. Well, and where's the harm? Most likely he took shelter from the storm here. Don't get involved, I remind myself.

Let him be. What you don't know won't hurt you.

I'll go down now and pretend I haven't seen a thing. He'll wake none the wiser, and be up and on his way. Nothing to explain, nothing anybody need account for. Let well enough alone.

But I look him over before I go, wondering whether he might be cold. Hair looks a little wet. He's wearing this thin summer shirt, old shirt, too snug at the shoulders. And his jeans are highwaters, a clear inch of ankle showing. Still lengthening out, I'd say. He'll be quite tall when he's done.

He isn't wearing any socks. Don't know how sensible that is. Judging from his shoes, he's been on the go for a while. They're running shoes, blue once with white stripes, but now so gummed with grease and scuffed and battered, you'd never know. And the treads are worn smooth. Sure, he's been on the run. But there's no packsack or anything — I feel around to make sure.

That tan, now! It's more a sort of light coming from him. Golden. Like he's been working out in the air all summer long. On one of the mail boats maybe, you get a good burn on the water. But his hands don't look rough like they would be if he'd been hauling traps. It's just that glow he's got that puts me in mind of sun on water.

Could be fever, though. I wonder. I'm afraid to touch and wake him, so I stoop near and listen to his breathing one last time. Curls so tangled . . . I lean over: his breath feathers my cheek: it's cool. Even. His breath coming and going, quiet and measured. Hair so damp, wonder why. His eyes must be gray, I think, color of the sea when it's clouded; don't know why I think so, but I'm almost willing to bet on it. Something just tells me. There's a smell of brine about him, sour and salt.

Fast asleep. But one ear's hatched out, like he's listening. For a minute, I think he's faking — but that's crazy — his breathing's so regular, I know he can't be. I'd have scrammed if I thought there was the least harm in him.

He doesn't stir, not even when I start down, not even when I close the door and open it again on the sly; even then, he doesn't bat an eyelash. "Sleep tight," I say. "Not to worry. You're safe here."

Let him wake when he pleases.

Rounds

There's a little breeze stirring as I set out. It keeps me company, nice, about halfway into town, a sort of steady stroking. Then I lose it. By the time I get to town, the sun is bright. Up ahead, a maple turning, sets the eyes on fire. It's going to be a hearty day, too hearty by half — I'm buoyed up by the change, but I don't count on it to last.

I stop first at the town mooring. It's died down now, what little wind there was. Nothing much doing here: some people standing around, talking about the storm, what blew down, what's standing, what washed in. They've put up a sign near the dock:

5 MILES PER HOUR
WATCH YOUR WAKE

Flat calm. I stand awhile gazing out over the water, my eye skimming. The sea so quiet . . . hard to imagine where all that ruckus came from. I can hear the two-way radios on the lobster boats, coming through loud and clear. Giving the gulls what-for: "Get away, you damn shitpokes!" — everything normal. And Ma Fiddle on the CB telling all and sundry what she ate for breakfast — eggs, the bacon done nice and brown and crisp, who's leaving the island today, and how she's got a doctor's appointment at half past one. She's got stones, won't say where. Reminding her boys to steer clear of the fog bank off the Thrumcap and be home before dark. Everything so normal, it's hard to believe. Somebody's found a hornpout in a tub of haddock — must be a joke.

The sea is smooth, stroking.

The sky is very big today. Not a cloud, not a puff, not a feather. I stand for a while, just basking.

I'm doing my regular run in reverse. I pass the Commons, hurry on by the statue, the bench. No one I know, but I wave anyhow, none answering. I notice they're boarding up the band shell: the Department of Public Works truck parked on the lawn in front of it. Everything looks a little windbent, beaten. One of the big old trees is down; they'll have to take it with a chain saw.

At Mullins', I stock up. Monday's always a big day, fresh deliveries and since I don't shop on Sundays. And today it's more than usual: spaghetti, head of lettuce, tomatoes, pound and a half of apples — they're good now. I'm not going by a list today, I'm making it up as I go along. Loaf of bread, milk, two beers, bottle of Coke, doughnuts, chips — just in case. In case — what? If he woke up and stayed a while, what would we have to say to one another? Anything at all? I doubt it.

"Nice day!" It's Mullins in the milk and butter.

"Hard to believe, isn't it?" I say.

I race through checkout, taking another girl, the one with the frizzed hair and all the rings on her fingers. The line's shorter here. I've got my back to Sue, so I can't tell if she looks up or even notices. I doubt it.

Home

It's full morning now, a razzle-dazzle day. Indian summer
all over again, I think. But no — the wind's struck up afresh,
the leaves are blowing. The leaves are starting to let go.

My shoulder's stiff. I stop off at the mailbox: nothing.
The front yard's full of cranberry, checkerberry, and hare-
bells, I guess you call them, those little blue drooping bells.
Wild stuff: weeds, stubs. The grass gleams, but darkly, it's
still wet. House looks pretty nice, coming up on it like this,
like a stranger might. Looks cozy: neat as a capsule, tucked
away in its pocket of pine.

Soon as I open the door, I'm curious. Want to open all
the doors and shout: Anybody here? Anybody home? But of
course there's no one. I stash the perishables in the fridge,
and, leaving the rest of the groceries on the table for later,
I'm on my way, my hand's on the door —

When I stop and think: wait! Wait just a minute. Say to
myself: he's there or he isn't. If he's already gone, what am
I hurrying for? If he's still up there, what's the rush? Have
a bite first. And if he's still sleeping the way he was, might
as well take something along to help pass the time. Like that
book I was in the middle of. Then I can stop up there for a
while, stay on till he wakes. He'll probably want to find the
route to the bridge right away. In a tearing hurry, they always

are. So I'll just sit up there and wait for him. He might get lost if I don't.

Speaking of hurry: I make myself a cheese sandwich and find myself standing over the sink to eat it.

Halfway up the ladder, I stop and rest a minute. I'm not really tired, but it can't hurt. Still no problem in clambering up. I may not be as nimble as once I was, but I'm more careful now and that makes up for it.

He's still at it. He hasn't changed places, only shifted sides. Still breathing? I stoop over him. The same. Same as before. Bending now, I'm trembling a little, I'm bending years back, putting my ear to Helen's stomach when Davey was inside, hearing a new sound, like somebody knocking — muffled, but not letting up, like steps — soft, small, fast, far — far off but arriving.

His eyes seem to browse under their lids. They're open, a little, this thread of white showing. The whites seem to move, to move or melt as the light moves in them. But he doesn't blink. It's strange, but it can be done. Fish do it, sleep with their eyes wide open, drifting in slow circles, no lids to shut. What do they see? I wonder. Not water, but a dream of water?

It's so peaceful here. Becalmed. So far up, can't hear the rote at all. Of course, it's a quiet sea right now; we had our commotion last night. There's something scraping overhead, a thin sound. Birds on the roof, couldn't be anything else. Nothing else doing.

Never saw sleep like this sleep. *Look here* — I clear my throat, cough — *hey*! *What's the idea? Hey?* Don't know what to call him. No tags or anything. Must have a name. His running shoes say Adidas, so I could call him that. *Hey, Adidas, what am I to do with you? Got any plans?*

Where'd he come from? I wonder ... It's no use racking my brains, I'll have to wait to find out. I can wait, I've

brought up my book: it's something to do. In his own good
time. All I need is to find myself a comfortable place to sit,
some wall to lean up against. Over there — there's more
light. Don't need more than a patch. Might as well spread
out the mattress and sit on that, nobody else is using it.

Now then. Book's a bit mashed from my pocket. The
cover's bent back, let me straighten it first. Show some respect: a book is a book. There. That's it: *The Roman Caper.*
Picture of Whoosis — Milton Morrisel — on the back.
Leather jacket, billed leather cap, portrait of the author from
crown to crotch. Young fellow. Looks in pretty good shape
to me. Wrist peeking out — wants to show off his expensive
watch. Well, that's only natural. "A wonderful read," the
blurb says. Sounds like a "wonderful eat."

I'm on the eating part now, as it happens. "Marissa carefully picked out two filberts" — this must be my place. It
doesn't sound like anything familiar, not anything I've been
led up to, but it's been a while. Here's my marker, this little
arrow in the margin, so it has to be. It will come back to me
as I go along. ". . . an almond, a cashew, a scattering of salted
scattering of salted . . ."

I see the words I see them: "two filberts Marissa carefully . . ." Scatterings I see, the spaces between the words
that don't stay still. I focus hard but it's all coming undone
— words into letters letters into blots into specks into dust
in the eye. I rub my eyes, close them for a second. I am here
behind my eyes. My mind keeps humming. No words, no
tune to it at all, just humming. I open my eyes, try reading
it aloud: "a scattering of salted . . ." It doesn't make any
sense. Think: Marissa, two filberts. It still doesn't make
sense. The door's slammed between my eyes and my mind.

Force it open. Concentrate. *Push.* "Marissa carefully
picked out two filberts, an almond, a cashew, a scattering of
Spanish peanuts."

There! Was that so hard? The almond (I'm almost sure of it) is poisoned.

"She chewed slowly." Poor Marissa, poor fool! I'm holding my breath like I'm supposed to. As if that could keep Marissa from chewing. That's good, that's what they call suspense. " 'Will you have a little more sherry?' he asked. 'Why thanks, no, I...' " Keep your finger on it. Not *that* one — thumb's too big. Use the pointer — what do they call it? Index finger? That's why, for keeping track. That's better; or on the margin, isn't that better? The finger moves along and the print goes by in step. Little ruler, kind they sell at the five-and-dime, might be a help; I could keep it under the line I'm at to keep my eye from weaving.

I can hear my fingernail scraping as it goes along; it's *that* quiet. I'm hungry. But that's silly — I just ate. Power of suggestion, could be, those filberts and those salted — salted what were they? — a scattering of whatever, salted whatevers. Peanuts, I see it right here. Spanish ones. They're the little round kind, like spring peas. How I like them, when they're little and sweet. Where was I? Hungry. No, I've eaten, it was Marissa who just took a handful of nuts. Another thing: the butler asked Marissa if she wanted any more sherry. What was his name? Italian, wasn't it? Veni, Vinci... Veneti? Veneti, I think. It doesn't really matter. He just made the thumbscrew gesture behind Marissa's back — that matters, that's important. It's a clue, I think. Sure it is. He's not really a butler, but something else. Bartender maybe. Maybe not, the way he mixes and drinks the last drink of the evening alone... Up to no good. He'll look in on Marissa tonight, I'm willing to bet. Find the body cold or still warm or stiff or limp or —

Something.

And if he doesn't? Hmmm... what then? How about the chauffeur? Hmm? Who cares?

Who the hell cares?

"Why thanks no, I . . . no, I thanks no Why thanks . . ."
Stop blinking, that would help. "Will you have a little
more sherry?" She had it already; I read that before. Who
left the confession in the breadbox? If it isn't the butler
(who isn't a butler, remember), then how about the cook?
There, I . . . hmmm . . . I read mysteries, try to, because at
least they have a story like novels used to in the old days
and don't anymore. Beginning, middle, end — something to
keep you moving along. And I like to see the bad ones get
what-for, what they deserve, for a change. Like to see a little
justice in the world. "He bent a little lower." That's good:
I can see that, I see him leaning, falsely, this smile sticking
to his teeth. "Why Why thanks" — Again! Best to move on
from all this thanking, even if I do miss a couple of words.

chewed slowly thanks

Oh hell! It's the same business: my eye floats back and
forth, weaves without weaving anything. It's like that picture
I saw in Davey's social-studies book. Look at it one way:
you get two profiles kissing; blink a minute: and it's a table
with only one leg or one of those pedestals they put little
statues up on. Stare at it hard: it flickers back and forth
till you're dizzy: kissers, table, kissers. Depends on whether
you're looking at people in space or the space between
people.

How about if I closed my eyes for a whole minute? If I
rested them. Two minutes, a little breather. I could chant
to myself, one of those Indian words — *Om*, is it? *Ram
Nam*? A nice *round* sound. *Ram Nam, Om* . . . Or say something that doesn't mean much, like — like what? Most anything. Like: Once upon a time. Once upon a time and a
very good time it was . . . That's how stories used to begin.
In the old days, when they *were* stories.

Keep the eyes closed and try thinking of nothing. Trouble is, I can't think of nothing — it's always something. I can *say* "nothing" — but what I get is a picture — like, a truck-load of furniture being whisked into a black sack. Right now, I say to myself "nothing" and I get a picture of tunnels, all the tunnels, the hollow spaces in my head. Looks like that ad for nasal spray. Or, again, I say "nothing" and I think: "hungry" — right now I'm hungry. But I'm not really hungry, I can't be. Just empty.

But I do *feel* hungry. I open my eyes and the print swarms. The meaning's all come loose, floated off. Could be maggots swarming. That does it. So long, *Roman Caper!* Some other time, maybe? Maybe — I doubt it. I'll just look at things. Read around, what's here around me.

Don't know how long I've been up here, could be a couple of hours. The sun's shifted, the shadows broadened out. There's this hush over everything.

My watch has stopped.

I don't think it's been stopped for long, only a few minutes or so. After three seems about right. I'll start it up now and make the correction by radio when I go down. It's a good watch, all I have to do is remember to wind it. Bulova: a good make with a second hand. Strap's pure sterling silver. It's what the company usually gives if you've been with them more than twenty years, less than thirty. Might have gotten myself one of the gold-plated kind if I'd stayed in the one place five or six more years.

Funny, how they're called "watches." Why? Because you watch? And why are girls of a certain kind called "tarts"? For the little pies? Or the taste, the sweet-sour aftertaste of them? Kind of silly — isn't it? — giving a man a watch right when he stops watching time. Might as well give him a silver-plated yo-yo, it's about twice as useful. It was only on company time that I really paid attention to time. Paying attention isn't the word: I breathed to the clock, ate to it, paced my digestion, tried to — it scrambled me up, often. Even my visits to the Necessary were ruled by it. Never forget Bill Hanson standing outside the stall and beating down the door: "Feeling all right in there, Will? Or just sitting and thinking things over?" And not even letting up when I told him I had legitimate business — nature's business — that couldn't be hurried. "Taking your time about it, Will, aren't you? I'm not the boss with the big stick. But it's nine o'clock. Thought you'd like to know."

Nine o'clock . . . that was strict starting time. We'd start, all right, saying good morning, sharpening pencils, stalling, but warming up to it, about ready to face it — after a sip of water, a little fussing with things on the desk. Then plunging into it with one thought in mind: coffee break, ten-thirty. And then it was easier, it wasn't so long a haul until lunch. Afternoons from one to five were the pits. No air, it felt, just this one gray pocket of it. Find myself staring off at the clock, the hands locked there, wishing so hard for the short one to fall. Seemed like it never would.

Quarter to five, near quitting time, how everybody perked up! It was a second wind, a big breath went through the whole room. The secretaries would begin brushing the eraser crumbs off their desks, taking great care, making sure all the little caps to all their little bottles were screwed on tight — mustn't get rusted out. They'd only peck at their keyboards then. Too busy getting ready: lining up their pencils in rows, peeking at the hand mirrors in their purses, touching up the lipstick, smoothing the eyebrows, filling in every fraction of the minute till it was time.

It was slavery, but it was something to hang on to.

It's three-forty now. And seventeen seconds, to be exact. Not that it matters to anyone here . . . How about it, boy? Nights are for sleeping, you know. And days are for —

I forget.

If they don't give you a watch at the end, it's something else about as useless. Like they did to that janitor. Simon. Can't forget that. Giving him a camera when everybody knew he had the shakes, his hands shook so it was plain as day he'd never get a clear shot. Yet he was gracious about it. Gives a little speech by way of thanks: "I don't believe anybody owes me anything." Must have rehearsed it. "My life is sweet... God's like the sun — He can't help but shine." Up there in front of all of us, going on and on. This great big fellow. "I tried to make the little things easier for people..." Ended up with — what was it? "Love and God bless." Something like that. Sappy coming from anybody else, but from him you could take it. Such a sweet fellow.

Wonder what he's up to now, right at this moment. That little party would be more than five years back. Odds are, Simon isn't sitting up a tree talking to the air. For I *am* talking to the air: the boy still hasn't stirred, the shade has moved up from his feet, crossed his long shanks, touched his shoulder. Wonder what sort of voice he has, whether I'll ever hear it. Just changing, I'd imagine, swooping up and down.

Sleep seems as heavy. It's quiet here. Quiet everywhere. There isn't anywhere else, it feels. We're drifting. The place moves when the wind strikes up. Sways us, this soft bumping motion, drifts us. This slow sidewise S. Something rises, something falls. Like a sailor's watch, a lookout, atop a high mast. The rigging creaks. It's blowing now, so I think for a moment I'm diving down.

Still blowing. Maybe I am a little giddy, after all.

We're rising now, we're surely rising, riding a current of air. Sailing, but anchored down. I *hope* we're anchored.

How young he is, how nourishing his sleep... Looks

positively blessed. It's not as if he's sleeping something off; there's no strain in it at all.

Like a baby. Davey used to sleep like that, then he lost it. Can't remember when that was exactly. Must have happened little by little. Wonder how you lose it once you have the knack?

I should report this to the police right away, I guess. No, I know I should. I really should. He's just a kid, a minor, after all. If his sleep were the least bit labored, the least bit strained, I would, if he seemed drugged. But he's sleeping so pretty, seems a pity to interrupt. So peaceful it almost drowses me, a little.

And, say, he's run away from someplace, say he's in trouble? I can't help thinking how he might be. So it's best to wait a little longer. Get the story straight from him, first. If he's not up by tomorrow morning at the latest, that's another story. Then I have to turn him in.

Meantime, the sandman's got him. How does that go? I can't remember how that worked, whether the sandman poured sand in your eyes and made them so heavy you couldn't open them, or whether he made them grainy and aching so if you didn't close them you didn't sleep.

Can't recall any of those bedtime stories, either, those that Davey was so keen on once. I can never remember where it was that the Pied Piper led all those children off to. It wasn't good, that I do know.

And who was it that slept for hundreds and hundreds of years? Some king, banished, gone away and waiting it out till his hour would come. I forget his name. Happened so long ago. Some king sleeping in a cave in the side of a mountain somewhere. Germany, I think. I'm not sure. Every few centuries, he'd wake up to give his beard a hack, saw off his nails. And he'd send his valet out to scout, to report on what was doing out there, what the weather was like and all. When the valet came back, the king would ask: "What time is it now?" And the valet: "Noon, sire." And the king: "Too early yet, we'll have to wait a while," so he'd turn in for another couple of centuries. After a few more hundreds of years, he wakes up again and inquires: "Tell me, valet, do the swallows fly over the mountains still?" And the valet: "Sire, they do." And the king: "A little patience, then." And he turns in once more.

How come I remember that one? Doesn't make a bit of sense, can't remember the point of it, if it had any, but I can still see that king's beard branching out like a river of weeds, curling and twisting itself around sticks and stones, snagging on everything in sight. Some things don't leave me.

Guess my memory isn't that bad. Patchy, is all.

So many stories ... It didn't matter how they started — whether it was "One very fine day," or "In olden times, when wishing was some use," or "Hard by a great wood," you could almost always trust them to end with "happily ever after" — everything looking rosy. So it would be all right for the kids. Only a few ran to the bad. No matter how awful things got in the middle, you could trust them to turn it round in the end.

But it was all lost on Davey. How he used to press me! "Go on, Daddy, what happened after that?" I'd try and explain: "Nothing happened. That's the end. That's what 'happily ever after' *means* — the same amount of happy, day in and day out." But even then, that wasn't enough for Davey: he wanted his happy with interest compounded.

It's all so slow, the light slowly seeping away, the shadows gaining. The boy stretched only a minute ago. He's shifted to his other side. I'm waiting for some follow-up, but there hasn't been any. What could be passing in his mind? Sleep that smooth, could he be dreaming? Wish I had a movie of his mind.

He's moved his hand, it's fallen over his belt; a shadow, branch shadow, crosses his mouth, brushes his eyelid, beats there, or that's a pulse beating. He takes one noisy deep breath. Then back to how he was. His teeth look small and sharp, wolfish, in this light that's always changing.

Now his arms are bunched across his chest, like he might be a little chilly. I'll bring up a blanket if he doesn't wake soon. Or better yet, a coat; I can wear it up and keep my hands free. And I'll put a few things in the pockets. Might as well get going now. Any longer and I'll forget I'm alive. Already I'm numb, stiff as a board from sitting in one place so long.

I'll hear him if he comes down while I'm eating supper. Bowl of chowder or minestrone, now, wouldn't that be nice? When he wakes, I'll hot up a plate of soup for him. Before he goes.

Moonlight

Phone's ringing. I can hear it, starting from before I touch the ground. Wrong number, probably. It's no use hurrying; I'll never make it in time.

Clam chowder tonight. I sop it up with bread and butter. Start wandering, wondering — my mind rambles so — what does it mean: "happy as a clam?" Closed-up happy? Complete?

No coffee. It's too late. I keep thinking of Davey, why don't I enjoy him more and when did I last? *I* haven't changed, I don't think, but he has. Once he was loving, pert, sharp as a tack.

Like dreams: only a tot then and trying to explain. Something he thought he'd discovered. "When I sleep I see pictures," he says. "*Dark* pictures." And the questions he asked! Like "ironic." All of five years old and already asking: "What's 'ironic' mean?" Damned if I knew, myself. Tried to give him some sort of answer, best I could, something about being funny and sad at the same time. What was it he said back? "Oh, I know..." he was smiling, big smile, so proud of catching on. "I know — like dying standing on your head!"

It's still fresh in my mind. Such a bright boy. Sweet, too.

Why did he turn on me? Did the best I knew how. It's
something that happens, that's all. Same as with kittens:
they get to be cats; the time comes, it's nobody's fault.

And now . . . We don't see eye-to-eye on anything. Not
one blessed thing. Take money, for instance: what's money?
Something — a lot, if you don't have any. But not everything. Health is everything, you can't *buy* health! But no,
he thinks there's some magic in money. Now, I'm comfortable. Put something by every day of my life. Thrift, it pays
off. I don't lack for anything money can buy, but what
have I got? When all's said and done, what have I *got*?
Look at Howard Hughes: call that a life? So rich and so
pinched, poor as poor can be. Lived in a tube, for all prac-
tical purposes. Davey never had to do without, and he earns
enough now — why should he crave for more? Why? Working nine to five isn't clever, isn't daring enough — it's got
to be quick, big money. Always some bright scheme. The
Pyramid Club, that's only the latest. I tell him like I always
do, "You'll lose it, it's money down the drain. You'll see."
But no, not him: "I can't lose. It won't fail. It's based on
greed, Dad, something you can always count on."

When did I teach him that?

We push into each other's lives. Nothing comes of it but
backing up. I ought to know. It was the same with me, I
always was a big disappointment for Dad. I knew it, he
knew I knew it, we didn't pretend any different. He wanted
me in the army, that was life, a man's life, all the rest was
sitting on the porch — fit for women maybe. Last thing I
wanted was to be anything like him. Might have been the
same with Dad and his Dad, for all I know.

I stack the dishes in the sink. Quick rinse-over, in case
I'm back late. I have a feeling I might be. It's a long nap
he's taking but I'm going to try not to worry over it. I heard
about a fellow who lived through a shipwreck once. Waves

ran him up on shore; he was the lucky one, slept three days
and nights solid, so done-in, the rest all gone under. Never
was in quite his right mind after that, none too swift, but
he lived. Three whole days and nights together! That was
a far case, of course.

Leave the kitchen light burning, so I don't have to make
my way down in the dark. Slip on my nylon windbreaker,
that ought to be enough for me. Old coat over that, to
cover the boy with if he's cold. Then I close the door behind me and start out, my heart coasting.

It's quieter and quieter as I mount up. I'm overheated,
eager to shed my top layer, and I do — soon as I'm up and
inside.

Needn't have hurried. He's still sleeping.

I've brought up a flashlight on a bicycle clip. I'll leave it
here when I go. It latches onto the leg so his hands can
be free — he can figure that out. I'll have to remember to
keep up a rhythm when I go laddering down in the dark;
it'll be all right, I'll inch it, keeping count, is all.

I'll just leave the overcoat beside him. "Are you cold?"
I ask. He doesn't answer, of course. "Sleep — sleep your life
away, it's your life. Don't mind me," I say to the air. I take
the doughnuts out of the pocket and set them down beside
him. He'll be hungry when he wakes. Any day now —

You'd think he had all the time in the world. Never saw
anything like this. Only Helen near the end, but that was
different, that was coma, not natural. "Stroke," they called
it. That's what they say when they're stumped, when something strikes somebody out of the blue. What do the doctors
know? Bunch of bandits, if you ask me. "We don't expect
her to wake up," they said. "Why don't you get yourself a
magazine, a cup of coffee? She can't hear you now." How
did they know? I used to talk to her all the time. That's
when all this talking started. I wanted to say it all, all the

never-saids, wanted to make up for all the blank times. First time in my life I ever was a talker, when it was no use. Guess I thought it just might be. I kept on talking so she wouldn't feel alone, even if she couldn't answer. Or in case she *was* playing games, or testing me; half the time I secretly thought she was. I was practically begging: "Helen, what's my name? Open your eyes, Hel. Look at me. Just once, come on, Helen. I know you can do it. For me." But she never did.

She was getting set to vanish. I held her hands, tried to hold her back. Didn't wish her a good journey, didn't want her to go. "If you hear me, press my hand, Helen. *Try!*" I made a lot of noise, but I had to. Kept right on talking because my teeth would chatter if I stopped. And there was something I didn't want to hear, a most particular sound, coming from those curtains on frames they put up around certain beds, the sound of the metal clips of those curtains bunching and spreading. I had to drown it out.

"Just once, try—" I'd say. If I said it once, I said it a hundred times. "It's me—Will. Don't you remember me? Will? What's my name, Helen?" She didn't answer. Not a word, not a signal. Never opened her eyes. All the memories—all that we'd lived through together—canceled. Who else could I tell them to? Our lives so mixed together now, how could I sort them out?

Times, I thought she heard me but couldn't be bothered. No way to tell. Her face said nothing, the lines smoothed away. Erased. She looked younger than she'd ever been before. Even the fingerprints go in the end, they say.

But the boy's sleep isn't anything like that.

How do I know? I don't, really. Seems perfectly natural, the way he breathes, way he holds his fingers, loose, sort of spilled out. I do wonder, though. About his getting up to take a leak every now and then, for one thing. Wonder how he . . . ? Must somehow. But the coffee can is dry as a bone, so I know he hasn't used that. Guess he could just piss down the open door into the air. Like pissing into the ocean, I did that, got quite a thrill out of it when I was a kid. But he hasn't changed places, far as I can tell, so I don't think he's gotten up on the sly. Of course, he isn't drinking anything. Even so.

Hey, you — yoo-hoo — how about it? What am I to do with you? Tell me. Can't help wishing he'd open his eyes for once. Even for a minute. Then I'd be real for him, I'd be alive for him, we'd both be alive —

It's getting chill. Moon's up. Only a half, but great big and white. The shadows move in closer. It's a queer sad light, moonlight. Milky, no weather in it, a sort of steady doting. Monotonous. The boy sleeps, spooked, rinsed in it. His head is dark, but his neck and hand are bright. I can hear the pine needles move as the wind passes, the dry on the wet, sounds like, like whisks dusting water. And I hear leaves moving, the wind — thin water streaming. Night's full of these small sounds you hardly ever notice, they come out when it's quiet. When I move my arm, the cloth of my windbreaker squeaks; anyone could hear it. In this big hush we're in the middle of.

Still quiet . . . Not like Helen's last, not like the dead spaces when I try to keep a conversation going. Not gagged on this. This is flowing, clear and deep. The kind of clear people always rush in to muddy. Like that canyon when I was a kid in Nevada. Malorty, they called it. Nothing you'd ever want to pay to see. Deserted; not a sound there, except the wind passing through. Must have been like that for ages . . . peaceful. But the kids wouldn't let it be. Used to go down there, a bunch of them, and yell themselves hoarse. When they hollered out "Board of Health!" it came back "Go to hell!" Over and over, they never got tired of it.

But now his sleep is too heavy, I think, hair heavy, still looks soaked so long after the rain. Something steps out from him to me, from me to him. His hand shuts, opens, steps my way. What are you after, hand?

I could swear we've been here before.

Haven't I seen you before? Couple of summers back? Might have been way back, the summers all blend together now. Can't think when it was, but wasn't it just like this? The moon stood over the steeped roof, heel of my hand in the sky, not far, like now. You, sleeping away there like a picture of sleep. Or — was it? — was I the sleeper then, asleep in my time? I was young once, moved through my days in a dream, in a daze. And now it's over, turned around: you sleep; I watch and wait, my eyes won't shut at all. While you've been dreaming, I've been talking to you, telling you what I see. And you — not listening. You never listen, never have.

It's always been like this.

But I'm getting tired, chilled. Better cover him with the coat and go down. It's so quiet. Everything nodding off but the sea. And the moon, the half of it.

Sleep, then.

Hear that? I give you till morning.

Morning

Soon as I wake, I remember something in a dream about a treehouse. Then I remember it wasn't a dream. What I dreamed was that I'd gone to sleep on the roof of the house. And I feel cold and stiff, as if I'd done that, not dreamed it. It's hard to tell one thing from another at times, living alone so much. Think I've turned on the stove sometimes, and, as if thinking were enough to do it, I give myself five minutes for the water to boil. I'm always jolted when I find it cold.

Funny about the light in dreams. It isn't sunny, it isn't cloudy, it isn't night, it isn't day . . .

I can hear the rote, march and countermarch. Same old thing. I tip the shade, peek out: what's doing? Nothing; the same. Same as yesterday and the day before: bramble, privet, and the big oily leaves of the rhododendron, all standing in place. G'morning. Sun's in and out. I catch the shine of ocean for a minute, then all goes dull. Looks windless. And fairly dry — that's different from yesterday.

G'morning.

I'm rumpled and unfresh, surprised to find I've gone to sleep in my clothes. Like I've been on call. I'll take a shower, a warm one, then dress. I lay out fresh clothes beforehand. A flannel shirt — I'm fairly chilled.

What is it about water, water on the head, that brings out the voice? Or is it because nobody hears? I catch myself humming an old tune — "Pins and Needles in My Heart." Ma used to sing that; that and "Believe Me If All Those Endearing Young Charms" were her favorites, as I recall. But she never sang of a morning. "Sing before breakfast and you'll cry before noon," she'd say. Still, that's better than weeping all day long. And anyhow, I can't stop it, the voice just wells up.

I tear through breakfast, I'm eager to get going.

It's bleary out. Kind of bleak, air's kind of raw. The sea's gray this morning, the water clouded, color of flint or gun metal — or darker, the metal of bells. It puts me in mind of winter. A flannel shirt feels just right for now.

There are webs all over the grass. Wonder when that stops.

I'm close to the tree — then I hear it. Stopped cold: it's something queer. Something driving up. Comes barreling up the driveway. Maybe it's backing, I hope so.

No . . . it's parking.

It's parked, he's getting out of the truck. He's all blue, some sort of uniform, he's starting to nose around.

Better go see.

"Morning!" he calls as I come round the bend. "Morning," I call back. His truck's got the name of the phone company blazoned on the sides; my old company, New England Telephone, but another branch. Must have some business being here. "Nippy, isn't it?" he says, his eye roving, "I near froze this morning." I agree it's real autumn now. "Getting fixed to rain," he points to the sky. I don't look at it — it's too close. Stare at his chest pocket instead, got a badge on it, nameplate, tiny letters I can't make out. "What can I do for you?" I ask. It's a nudge.

"Look here," he smiles, "it's what can I do for *you*. Thought the post might of blown down." He points to the pole, then a little up and to the side, his finger floats a little in the air. "Somebody called in and reported your lines were down."

"How can that be? It's working fine."

"Well. I can't tell unless I take a look at it. Somebody did call. I'll just have a look, if I might — test it and phone in my report at the same time. Won't take but a minute."

I show him in and where it is. He's quick about it: like I say, nothing wrong. He crosses me off on this little pad he's got with him. "Don't know what your problem was. Could of been some temporary electrical interference, night of the big storm . . ." I notice he's oiled his hair; I used to do that. I mention that I worked for the phone company myself once, don't know why I bring it up. Just to seem friendly, I guess. A friendly sendoff. I want to be off so bad my toes are clenched with it. His eye's wandering again. I tell him that was years back, quite a number of years, I'm talking too fast. "That so?" he says, not too terribly interested. I know what interests him. He glances at it, then away over the grounds. "Nice place you've got here."

I nod.

"See you've got a treehouse."

Nod again, like nothing's going on.

"Looks unsafe to me. I wouldn't let any kid of mine play up there. First off, it's way too high."

"That's my business, isn't it?" Voice just rushes out of me. I check myself, take a long breath: go easy. Soon I'll be shouting how it's a free country, if I don't watch it. "You know," I say, casual as I can, "place hasn't been used in years and years."

"All the more reason for taking it down, don't you think? Just a friendly suggestion. Why get excited? If anything happened, you might have a lawsuit on your hands. You wouldn't want that. Or worse — it could happen to somebody in your own family."

"I'll see to it."

He tells me he knows a carpenter from someplace. Think I hear him say Grand Speck, but that can't be. Maybe Grant's Pass, I've heard of that. Just said his name. I'm fussing over the place, and I missed the fellow's name!

"I'll keep him in mind," I say. It isn't easy. My mind's evaporated, flown clear off. It isn't with me. I'm winding my watch, don't realize I'm doing it till his eye halts on me, I catch his eye on me, steady, and I notice the little itch of sound. I look down at my wrist. Don't dare look up at the tree. He's staring off at it again, gazing, not saying a word. "Got to get cracking," I announce. "Got things to do in town."

"I'll jot down his name for you. He'll do a nice clean job of it and it won't cost you a fortune either."

"Oh, thanks, don't bother. Thanks just the same."

"Only take a minute. Might as well give you the phone number while I'm at it."

So I wait.

"There. That's all there is to it. Same area code," he hands it over.

"Well, that's very kind of you," I say, about to be really grateful now, thinking it's over, he's on his way. He steps up to the truck: "Don't lose it!"

"I won't." I fold the paper into thirds and tuck it into my shirt pocket. Give the pocket a little pat for good measure.

"Maybe I'll have him give you a ring. To be on the safe side."

"I'll take care of it, I'm telling you."

"Wouldn't be any trouble — he's an old friend of mine."

"I said I'd take care of it. I won't forget — thanks a million!"

"All right..." He settles into the driver's seat, slams the door. Starts up the motor; leans out: "Can I give you a lift anywheres? You said you were going into town."

"Oh, no — Thanks anyway. I need my exercise — it's important, get to be my age. We have to go on living, you know. See your way all right?"

He waves: fine. Fine: I wave him out. He gives a glance to the treehouse as he turns: "Don't wait!" I wait a minute — minute I turn my back he might just — I can't take a chance on it. Better count ten ... One: that's to the paved road. Two: it's a bit broken up but he's not going fast, shouldn't be. Three: slowing down at the fork; four: on, and someways over the bridge; five, six: passing the WATCH OUT FOR CROSSWINDS sign; seven, eight: over the bridge, nearly over; nine: turning left into town. Ten: I'm on my own. Feel like clapping: eleven: gone! I'm safe. I'm safe, I think. For a little while at least. I turn on my heels and head straight for the tree. No one stopping me now.

I clamber up, threading my way through the branches. Well, here's hoping —

What? What am I hoping?

Hello?

He's still there, still in the same place. I'm about certain it's the same: lying on his side, face turned toward the entrance, but he's shifted position, one arm flung out to the side. Looks warm, his forehead's damp. I peel back the overcoat and set it aside. He stretches, like I've lifted off a weight; heaves, his arm sweeps over me. Hand brushes my cheek. Softside, but I'm stung. I rock back on my heels, stabbed with surprise. My ear ringing. "You awake?" I ask, my voice scratchy, a whisper. I'd think he touched me on purpose, but when I back away, his hand thuds down so loud it must hurt, and I know his sleep is heavy.

A stab — that hand. Same as the last time with Dad. When Dad died, he was putting up his arm — I'll never forget it. Shocked me so. He died with his right arm raised up. I'd stiffened, backed away, certain he was going to strike me. I was sure at the time: I backed up sharp when I should've taken his other hand. So stunned. Thinking back, I know what it was. He was trying to give a salute — to give someone or something a salute. Nothing to do with me. I wasn't there for him at all.

The boy gives a wheeze, a low whistle in his throat, but doesn't stir again. What to do now? The doughnuts are still beside him. There's a tiny brown nip in one of them, but it's about a tooth-and-a-half wide. Only a squirrel could have done it. The flashlight is in the exact same place I left it, the coffee can dry as a bone.

This can't go on.

But what? What am I waiting for? Today I've got to turn him in. Longer I wait, the harder it gets to explain.

But I do wait, because I have this feeling he's not sleeping as deeply as before. Don't know why I think so . . . a shift in his breathing, maybe. There — hear it? A definite speeding up. The smooth's broken, the rhythm uneven now. And his lashes — they're moving.

Keep on feeling I'm not alone, he's watching me, the whites of his eyes, what I catch of them, glinting sharp. How the blind see, secretly. I have that feeling I get when somebody blind turns his blank eyes on me, this feeling of being undressed. They miss nothing, blind eyes, but coats and covers and wraps. This white that scours you down.

His hand shifts from thigh to chest, seems to drift, float. Then drift back again. The minute I think he's starting to wake, he settles back. Still, I wait.

I wait, but nothing really changes. And then his breathing slackens off. Sleep seems even deeper than before.

Not even a ripple now.

That's that! Now I've got to do it. Every minute I delay,

I'll be more and more to blame. Trouble enough already explaining why I waited this long.

How long? A day and a night, and now today. That's counting from when I found him. No saying how long he's been here before that. And it seems, it feels so long ago, my first coming up here . . . how can I be sure? Better get a paper first: check the date. And — somebody might have posted a notice. It's worth looking.

Quick glance at the paper, then I'm bound to report him. I could maybe say I found him today. Or last night, that wouldn't be too far off. I'll do that. Who's to know? Nobody around to say any different.

The White Cup

I stop first at the harbor. That storm I can't forget is ancient history by now. Thought there might be a wreck or something washed up since, but nobody's mentioned a thing. An old fisherman is standing on the wharf shouting down to a young one: "Day like yesterday, now, you're sure the catch's gotta be good ... It's a funny trade, though. Some days you think you're gonna be a rich man, and some days you think you're gonna starve. But you won't do either one."

I'm listening for something. Don't quite know what it is, but I'd know it once I heard it.

It's not here.

Over there, I think — that bench at the narrow end of the park, that'd be quickest. I'll sit down only a minute. There's nobody near.

This is fine. No distractions here, nothing to look at but the boarded-up band shell and a long stretch of stubble the summer's whitened. It's going to rain sometime soon. Along about afternoon, I expect. I've bought the local rag, something I hardly ever do, so I'm not much familiar with where things are. Bird cholera along the southern coast, I see. It's in the Classifieds, I think, I'll find what I'm looking for, if I find it at all. But I'm not really sure: I'll have to keep my eye peeled.

Invitation to a casserole, bring your own forks ... A poem by Harold Vinal about the interminable sea. "Interminable" seems pretty correct to me.

Mustn't forget to check the date —

Tuesday. That's all right, then, that's not too long. Feels long, though. "The Merrylakes fishermen got all of the big ones." I'd better home right in on the Classifieds. Must be in the second section. Here we are. For Sale ... Services ... Real Estate, Boats ... I'm wasting time. Wanted — that's more like it. Let's see.

> "Always Buying ..."
> "Anything Old ..." Things, they mean.
> "Will Pay Top Dollar ..." No.
> "Old Coins ..." No.
> "Used refrigerator ..." No.

No. I'll just keep scanning. Help Wanted, Work Wanted, For Rent, Cards of Thanks, Miscellaneous — maybe ... No, nothing. Lost — aha! — that's more like it —

But it's only two lines and I can tell at a glance that it's nothing helpful: "Johnson Seahorse 5½ HP ... Fuzzy brown and white ..."

So that's it. My course is clear. Has to be. I'm folding the paper up, when what should I notice? On the front page, too, staring me in the face. But it's at the bottom of the page, in tiny print. Kind of thing I've been looking for all along:

> *George to Mary. Come home please.*
> *I miss you. Kisses to Mikey.*

That's all. Just the one notice. I know what I have to do.

But my feet are slow at it. I'm stiff, rusted out. It's the damp in the air, plenty of it. And — oh, no — I'm rounding the post-office corner on my way to the police station at last, and — I don't believe this! It's the damndest thing.

"Will! Oh, Will —" She starts waving and hallooing from half a block off. "Wait up!" It's Lil Harmon. I lift my hand in reply and move on forward to meet her, there's nothing else I can do.

"What a coincidence! I was thinking of you all the way coming into town. I've been calling to let you know." We're standing close to where I ought to be. "Tried calling you right after the storm. You don't know how many times I picked up that phone. Kept getting no answer — I got worried. Then I called the phone company to check whether you'd been blown over."

"So it was you."

"I was worried."

"Phone's fine."

"Seems like you're never in, then . . . Don't let's quarrel, Will. How are you? How've you been?"

I can see the steps of the police station over her shoulder. Looks like I could put out my hand and touch those steps, so close. And still so far! Find myself staring at Lil's ear: it's nice, fits close to her head, small and neat with these tight little whirls to it. She's pressing both my hands. "Only been a day or so," I say.

"What's new?"

"What could be new?" I turn the question round, and when she sighs I know I'm in for a long answer. I'll have to wait for it, she'll dole it out, particle by particle, I know it. "So . . . what brings you down here?" I begin.

"I'm buying a mess of those pine pillows. You know, the ones that smell so nice. They make nice gifts. I'm going off in a week, I've decided." She looks up at me, her eyes very full, her lids very blue. "Maybe for good."

"Really? You said you were going off, but why so sudden?"

"I told you when I saw you I might. I had this offer, I

was thinking it over. I hadn't made up my mind then. But now I have. Maybe that storm decided me, I don't know. It means I'll lose a couple weeks sublet, but it's worth it. I think it's worth it..."

"I didn't know it would be so soon," I say. I'm not forgetting — but what else can I do? — I invite her to stop with me for a cup of coffee. "Can't sit but a minute," I say. I haven't forgotten. In my mind's eye, I see him as he was. I see him slowly stir and stretch. Was he only settling down again, as I thought? Or struggling and falling back, but starting to wake? I hadn't the patience to see it through.

We stop in at The White Cup, the place nearest by. It isn't elegant, but it will have to do. We sit in a little booth for four. I order a cup of chowder and a Danish. Might as well be efficient with my time. It's only coffee for Lil. Already eaten, she explains.

"You look pretty well," she looks me up and down, sounding doubtful.

"I'm not ill, but maybe a little tired," I have to admit.

"Tired? From what?"

Oh, from resting, I'd say if I could speak the truth, it's resting really gets you tired, I need a rest from resting. "Been running," I explain, "been running up and down."

"Well, take it easy then."

It comes to me: that hand — it was no accident... I'm trying to listen to Lil, really I am, something about beet juice, if I hear aright. Warm milk and horseradish for the liver. It's hard to concentrate. A car barks up the street. A clock, must be somewhere back of my head, clicks, gears up to move a minute. I can hear the wheels humming. My ear's ringing — his hand just missed my ear.

She's laughing a little — I don't get it. Something I missed? Did I miss the joke?

"You haven't heard a word I'm saying."

"Oh yes," I say, "beet juice and horseradish."

"You don't look all that well, you know."

"Me?"

"Look worried. Off somewheres all boxed up in yourself." She empties the cup. "There's something eating you."

"Been eating perfectly well," I say. "Still got a little breadbasket, could do without."

"No," she shakes her head, stares. "I mean it. Time heals, Will, you'll see. Sooner or later it's going to happen. What everybody says *is* true. It'll be all right."

"Oh," I say, "I know. Time cures." Packs it all up, folds it all in. Everything. "Hell, I know that." She's still staring into the cup. "Gonna tell my fortune?" I say.

"What, from an empty cup?" She laughs her cooling silvery laugh. "If you want ... The white cup. Ah, let me see, let me see ... See lots of air here, lots of space. Plenty fresh air."

"Lots of empty, you mean? A lot of nothing?"

"Why do you stay on, Will?" She grabs my hand for a second, then lets loose. She stares hard into my eyes. Eyes touch: it's a fact. Hers do. Then back off. "I can't understand it. A slick educated fellow like you. You'll end up hauling traps. Or sitting on one of those benches."

"*Now*, Lil," I say, trying to sound firm. "Let's not" — I slap my hand flat out on the table, as if we'd been arguing it for days — "let's not go into *that* again."

"Only trying to help out, Will. Dear." The last word hangs in the air: she's testing it, trying it out. Too much space: it hangs and flaps there. I scoot right by — got to — got too much else to do. "So tell me," I say, and for a minute can't think of what. "Tell me about your plans." And she brightens as she does.

And then I say: "I really must."

"Well," she says, "if you have to."

"It's been real nice talking to you." I pick up the check, glance it over, start to slide out. "Nice we met up again."

There's a sign over the cash register: TIPPING IS NOT A CITY IN CHINA. I point it out to Lil, and we look at each other and laugh. She's got nice teeth. A good sort, really, good-hearted. She'll be all right.

That's that, I guess. We step out the door and stand a minute shaking hands. "This really is good-by," she says. "I don't expect to be down this way again."

"Guess it is, then. Guess this is it . . ." I put pressure into the handshake, but Lil looks a little miffed, so I add a peck on the cheek for good measure. Maybe she's angling for me to ask her to the house, but of course I can't do that. Got enough to explain as it is. "I won't keep you," she says.

"I hope things work out, Will."

"Take care now," I wait for her to take the first step. "Take good care."

Passing the post office, I glance back over my shoulder to make sure —

Nobody: coast is clear. That's the last of her.

Start up the steps and I'm halfway there when — wait — wait — Come to a dead halt, stopped in my tracks, my right foot a step higher than the left. Say to myself: What am I doing? Been tacking this way and that, wasting time. Bet the boy woke up and started on his way while I was gabbing with Lil. He came to me for shelter, after all. There's that to consider. If he's been in trouble and is safely on his way now, why should I be the one to set the police on his tail? Let me go back to the house first and check once more. The very last time. If he's still as he was, then I'm honor-bound to report him.

I make a sharp about-face. This time I'll be quick. Nothing will stop me. But I'm sure he was stirring. More I think about it, the surer I get. I can see him, sitting up, wonder-

ing whether he's dreaming or not, wondering where in the
world he's come to, trying to get his bearings. Must be
quite a shock, I imagine. Or could be he's already gone, up
and on his way. Been time enough for that.

All right, I'm decided. I'm on my way.

The sky's overcast. One cloud's balled up, too bright, giving a glare, the light squinting behind it — headachy, if you
stare straight at it. The rest, just clouds in rows, gray, gray,
gray. I see with uncommon keenness, like you do when
you're looking over a place you haven't really noticed in
some time, a place so familiar it's grown blurred. It's the
light.

Here comes a dog in a hurry. He flies right by, eyes front.
Some kind of spaniel or hound with those long drooping
ears. What's he after? One ear's loose, I'm struck by it —
pink and slick, flopped clear over, inside out. What time *is*
it? My watch is stopped again. There's a clock up on the
tower of the post office, I should've looked when I went by.
Maybe if I squint hard it's not too far... After one, is all
I can make out, there are too many leaves in the way. I'll
set my watch at one-thirty, that sounds about right, I can
fix it later.

The leaves are blowing.

Aloft

Home again. Quick stop in the Necessary. Here goes —

No time to lose: I head straight for the tree. Hand over hand, I mount up. Up and up — no sense of climbing now — but shedding, maybe, lighter and lighter as I go. I don't look out or down.

Dim inside. So shadowy, can't tell at first whether he's here or gone. Still, I don't want to shout. It's crazy, I know.

Empty.

Place looks empty: that's good. That's good news, isn't it? Let me just. Must've climbed too fast too steep. Here I'll. I'll sit right down. Wait for my head to.

The light in tatters.

And then I see: he's here. He's here! Sleeping still. But one arm's thrown over his eyes, like the light's begun to register. And his breathing's sort of ragged now, little snags and catches.

Moves, I think he moves. I lean over.

"Hey —"

Not loud, not loud enough to say "boo" and mean it, no heart in it at all.

"Hey!" He hears it, I think. "Come on . . . let's go." He bunches up curls close. Comes so close, I know he hears.

"You're making it hard."

And I don't know why I don't look at him when I say it. "You hear?"

Long breaths for answer, his sleep leveling out. Might as well be talking to the wind. All right, stay, we'll rest a minute. I can hear the wind, wind on water, his lips move, water on water, no words I know. I'm all in. No breath. It's the rushing around, why rush? I'll lie down only a minute.

Not a soul but us. I feel now soon, soon I

What?

It's dark of a sudden. A shivering fine darkness: rain. Hair touches my mouth. You spoke? So soft you'd think the rain, must be the rain. How dark. I thought I'd lost you. How dark it is. My eyes so heavy arms so heavy hands so full they cannot hold. Touch me. Why is your hair so cold?

Hello?

I'm high, far up, it comes back to me with the swaying
motion. High adrift...

Been raining in some, I'm cold, it's damp beside me. I'm
chilled through and through. I touch the damp — you there?
— reach out on all sides. Hello? The place feels empty.
Empty: I know it before I get up and start to move, one
hand on the wall. There's no one here. Not a soul.

No moon.

How dark it is. Must be the clouds. I move to the window to make out the hands on my watch, and can just
barely. Near midnight: I must have been sleeping for hours
and hours. When it's lighter, I'll go down and look for
tracks.

The boards creak in the wind.

Hello?

Someone out there calling my name? Or just calling?

Hello... Hello? I'm here.

About the Author

A. G. Mojtabai's previous novels are *Mundome, The 400 Eels of Sigmund Freud,* and *A Stopping Place.* She is Briggs-Copeland Lecturer at Harvard University, with time out currently for a Guggenheim Fellowship. Previously she was a Fellow of the Bunting Institute of Radcliffe College, lectured in philosophy at Hunter College, and on narrative fiction at New York University. When unavailable in New York City or Cambridge, Massachusetts, Ms. Mojtabai is usually to be found in Manset, Maine.